Where's the Quetzal?

An Empty-nesters Cozy Mystery: Book 2

Jen Dodrill

Scrivenings
PRESS
Quench your thirst for story.
www.ScriveningsPress.com

Published by Scrivenings Press LLC
15 Lucky Lane
Morrilton, Arkansas 72110
https://ScriveningsPress.com

Printed in the United States of America

Paperback ISBN 978-1-64917-448-2

eBook ISBN 978-1-64917-449-9

Editors: Erin R. Howard and Linda Fulkerson

Special thanks to Clay King and Ron Johnson, my Gulf Breeze High School English teachers, who taught me to think outside the box.

Chapter 1

I woke, panting and sweating, sheets twisted around my feet. Eight months since the murders and the Keatons' escape, and I still suffered from crazy dreams. I pushed myself up in bed and brushed damp hair off my face. I did not want to experience any of it again, the nightmares or the murders.

Kicking off my covers, I padded to the kitchen. Morning sunshine filtered through the window over the sink and left soft shadows on the tile floor. I opened the dining room curtains and the blinds covering the back sliding door. A flicker of excitement wove through me, sweeping away the remnants of my bad dream. Today was the day—my baby's baby shower.

A glance at the clock kicked me into gear. No time to waste. "Things to do. Get moving, woman."

I started the coffee, showered, and dressed. When I returned to the kitchen, my mother-in-law, Hazel, sipped from her favorite purple mug. Charlie Brown, CB for short, sat beside her. I stroked the silky gray Weimaraner's fur.

"Morning, Peg. Are you ready for today? To celebrate my first great-grandchild?"

"And my first grandchild. Shortie will be here any minute,

if you want to get dressed." I gestured to her nightgown and robe.

She clutched her robe closed and headed for her room, CB on her heels.

Hope fluttered in my belly when Shortie arrived. It might have even been love. But I wouldn't be the first to say it. Today wasn't the day to figure out our relationship.

"You look very handsome."

He winked and leaned down for a kiss. "Thanks. I like your shirt. It's ... colorful."

I held out my pink and blue tie-dye I'm-the-Grandma T-shirt. "Thanks. I thought it appropriate for the day. I made it myself." It had been a messy project, ending with pink and blue dye everywhere, which took forever to clean up. "Want coffee? We can watch TV until we need to put up decorations."

"Sure." He whistled at Roscoe, Hazel's yellow parakeet, then perched on the edge of my brown leather couch, purchased after the murderer broke in and slashed my old sofa to pieces last fall. I retrieved a mug from the cabinet, filled it, and picked up mine before settling in beside him.

Several commercials blared, followed by the newsman announcing, "Estelle and Roger Keaton, sought in connection with two murders committed last year, have been spotted in Pensacola. If you see them or have any information, please call the number below." The couple's pictures and a Crime Stoppers number appeared on the screen.

"They're back? How did they enter the country?" My nightmare flashed through my mind. No way. I did not want anything to do with the Keatons again.

Ever.

Acid burned in my stomach, and it wasn't from my coffee.

Shortie ran his fingers over his hair. "They must have sneaked in. They're aware they are suspects."

"Hazel!" I called to my mother-in-law, my tone sharp and shaky. I would love to protect her from the news, but she needed to hear this. The Keatons' return affected both of us.

She popped her head around the corner from her bedroom. "Yes? What's wrong?"

"The Keatons. They're here ... in town." Thinking about them stressed my brain and my heart. They'd hurt too many people.

Shock crossed her face, her eyes widening.

"Peg," Shortie said, an edge of anxiety in his voice. He stood, took my hands, and pulled me up. "You cannot be involved in this." His eyes filled with worry. "Please ..."

His fears were valid. First, Roger Keaton went to Guatemala, and then his wife left town. *After* she masterminded two murders of my birding group friends and threatened my and Hazel's lives. No one knew if she joined her husband in Central America or had gone elsewhere.

"But how can we not do something?" Hazel demanded. "If not for Estelle, Anna and Sylvia would still be alive. And Roger Keaton. All of Pensacola knows about him. He's like the black stain on our fair city." She crossed her arms with a disgusted huff.

My feelings went to war with the truth. Hazel was right. If it weren't for Estelle, no one would have died. I didn't want to be involved, but I had to do something.

Shortie's gray eyes bored into mine. "You want to search for them. I know how you are. Nope, not happening. You almost died last time." His words ended in a growl.

I wrapped my arms around his waist and squeezed. "Thanks for worrying about me. You're my favorite boyfriend."

I hoped for a smile, but he grimaced instead. "I have good reason to be concerned. You two are this dynamic duo determined to catch bad guys." He gestured between me and Hazel.

She interrupted him with a raised hand. "Chloe's shower is today, so let's put this aside for now. We can discuss the Keatons after."

Hazel had a point. We needed to lay out the food, decorate, and prepare the games. We had a big day ahead of us.

"I'll bring in the rocker. It's crammed in the back of my Jeep." He shut the front door more forcefully than usual, his frustration loud and clear.

I blew out a breath. I didn't want to start the day with this news, and I didn't want it to dampen the party. *It's time to focus, Peg.*

I dragged five wooden dining room chairs into a semicircle in the living room, took the sixth, and placed it in the corner by the back door. Pink and blue helium-inflated balloons bobbed in the breeze from the overhead fan. I grabbed their strings in one hand, climbed on the chair, found a solid stance on the worn seat, and eased up, my arms out to both sides for balance. "Hazel, can you hand me some tape, please?"

She stuck several pieces on my hand. "A stepstool would be safer, Peg. Your chair needs wood glue."

I stood on my tiptoes and stretched as far as possible. "Nah, I can manage. Besides, I don't own a stepstool." Balloons tangled over my head. I wadded the strings and mashed them into place. "See? Ta-da!"

Roscoe echoed my words, and I chuckled. Laughing while teetering on the edge of a chair didn't work in my favor. The chair wobbled, the front door opened, and the next thing I knew, I landed in Shortie's arms.

"Perfect timing." I kissed his cheek and burrowed my nose in his neck, inhaling his woodsy cologne. "Never thought catching me would be part of your boyfriend duties, did you?"

I tipped my head back and said to Hazel, "Roscoe's discovered a new word." The parakeet squawked again from his cage on my prized teak buffet, and my mother-in-law shot me the stink-eye.

"At least we know how he learned this one," she grumbled, still irritable after discovering last year's intruder taught him the expression, "Birds alive."

"Point taken." I straightened out my clothes when Shortie set me on my feet.

Hazel shook her finger. "You're about to be a grandmother. You shouldn't climb on things. Tell her, Shortie. She might fall and break a hip." She dragged the offending chair to where its mates stood.

"I'm not that old." I resisted sticking out my tongue and settled for wrinkling my nose.

"I don't have a dog in this fight," Shortie said.

"Coward." I winked.

He rubbed his hands together. "How can I help?"

My boyfriend, a master at distraction. "Decorations are up, and the living room is ready." I checked the time. "Let's put out the food. Everyone will be here soon."

"I'll get the games." Hazel marched off to her room.

Shortie leaned closer. His husky voice sent delightful shivers through me. "What's up with her? Her mood changed so fast."

I crooked my finger, and he followed me into the kitchen. "No idea. She's been like this for the last couple of weeks." I opened the refrigerator and passed him a veggie tray.

"It's been a long time since she moved in during the last hurricane. Has her roof been replaced? The news said the roofing business is finally catching up with claims." He placed the tray on the island and turned back for more food.

"Maybe so. I'll ask her. I've actually enjoyed her company,

so I haven't thought about it much." I gestured to the counter. "Let's put the food on both sides of the island for easy access."

We laid out the snacks—the veggie tray next to a bright yellow fruit platter, a slow cooker of yummy barbecue meatballs, and two plates of tortilla roll-ups stuffed with avocado, turkey lunchmeat, and cheese— and I saved room for the cupcakes Lauree, my neighbor and BFF, would bring.

Hands on his hips, he surveyed the spread. "Do we need anything else?"

"Oh, I forgot the chips and dips. Thanks." I poured tortilla chips into one bowl, ruffled potato chips in another, and set salsa and onion dip next to them. "Now we have everything we need."

He put his arm around me and kissed my temple. "You've done a good job, Grandma."

I rechecked the time. "Chloe and Tom should be here soon."

"You mind if I watch more TV 'till everyone arrives?"

"No, go on. I have presents to put out." I retrieved several cute gift bags in various sizes and gender-neutral colors from my room, placed them on the floor by the back sliding door, and tipped the vertical blinds halfway closed. "Too dark?"

He shook his head.

I eyed the piles of presents. "Can you help me for a minute? I have two more things to carry out."

"Sure you got enough stuff?" he teased.

"Wait until the baby is born. I'll buy more." I bounced on my toes. "I can't wait to find out the gender. I wish the baby cooperated on the ultrasounds and showed us, but this is exciting." He followed me to my room, where a car seat and stroller set sat beside a long, wrapped box.

He tapped it. "What's this?"

"A portable baby bed, of course. It's bulky. Can you carry

it?" I rolled the stroller to the living room. He lifted the present and propped it in the corner.

"Why do they need a portable bed?"

I chuckled at his confused expression. "They don't. It's for me. For when I keep the baby. I plan to be 'that' grandma." I made air quotes.

His eyes softened. "I can't wait."

I squeezed his arm, snuggled closer, and imagined us being Grandpa and Grandma to the little one.

Hazel appeared with an armful of pink and blue bags and boxes. She stopped and stared, her bottom lip jutted out. "You didn't save room for more presents. Where should I put mine?"

I rearranged my gifts, and she set hers down. When she finished, I hugged her, held onto her arms, and studied her eyes. Usually, they were sparkling blue. Now, they were dim, filled with tears, and her lips quivered. "Are you okay?"

"My roof is fixed." A hint of desperation crept into her voice.

"It's taken a long time."

She stepped back and wiped her eyes. "Yes. Can we talk about it later?"

I nodded, accepting her decision to postpone our discussion. We needed to chat about her plans and the Keatons after everyone left.

A pizza commercial boomed, and Shortie lowered the volume, then sat to finish watching the news. Hazel showed me the games she planned, and we laid them out on the table. After a few minutes, Shortie called to us.

"What is it?" Not more about the Keatons, I hoped. I didn't want to think about them anymore right now.

"They found another ship near the de Luna wrecks," he said. "An extra one, not attached to his group—a caravel. It's smaller and lighter than the Spanish galleons de Luna used."

In the 1500s, Don Tristan de Luna, a conquistador, sailed from Vera Cruz, Mexico, to the northwest Gulf Coast with twelve ships and over a thousand people in an attempt to colonize the Pensacola area. A hurricane wrecked seven of the ships. Rumors said a rogue ship tailing de Luna's fleet carried gold, silver, and gems.

"I hope they find treasure this time." Hazel's eyes brightened.

A knock at the front door interrupted us, and Shortie clicked off the TV. Chloe and Tom entered, oohing and aahing at the decorations. My oldest daughter glowed, her baby belly shaped like a basketball, sitting high. From my experience as a mom of three, she wasn't close to delivery.

Lauree rapped once on the door and entered with a tray full of pink and blue cupcakes. She set them on the island and greeted us all, adding a thorough rub of CB's silky ears and a click of her tongue at Roscoe.

"How many others are coming?" She took a hair tie from her wrist and tied her long brown hair into a messy bun. "They can park in my driveway if they need to."

"A couple of Chloe's friends. Carter and his girlfriend should be here any minute. I'll let him know." I peeked at the time.

"Why do you keep checking your watch?" Shortie asked.

"There's a surprise for Chloe. Should be here soon." I tapped its glass face and held it to my ear. "Good, it's working."

He frowned, but I kept my secret. The front door opened, and my youngest, Carter, walked in.

I hurried over, tugged him close, and kissed his cheek. "I'm so glad to see you." I ruffled his auburn hair. "You've grown this out some."

"Yep. Mom, this is Mary, my girlfriend." He slipped his hand into hers, both of their faces beaming.

I hugged her, and Carter introduced everyone else. When Chloe's friends arrived, Hazel waved them to the living room before escorting Chloe to the new rocking chair situated under the balloons.

She ran her hands over the gleaming wooden armrests. "This is perfect, Mom."

I pointed to Shortie. "It's his gift to y'all."

"Aww, thank you." She struggled to stand.

He hurried to her and leaned over for a hug. "You stay here. We don't want the baby coming today. You have another month, I think."

Tom chuckled and shook Shortie's hand. "Soon would be nice. Thanks so much."

"Not too soon," I mumbled, peeking at my watch again. The doorbell rang—perfect timing. A glance at Chloe showed her deep in conversation with her friends.

The door opened, and there stood my middle child, Cynthia. Her brown bob framed her heart-shaped face, and her blue eyes, so like her father's, sparkled.

"Hi, Mom." She wrapped her arms around me. "It's so good to be home."

I kissed her cheek and released her, fanning my face and blinking back tears. "It's been over two years."

"I couldn't miss the birth of my first niece or nephew."

I studied her. "You look good, Cynth."

Chloe gasped, interrupting our quiet moment. Carter's mouth dropped open, CB barked, and Roscoe screeched, "Ta-da!"

Chaos ensued, followed by hugs, tears, and more introductions.

Cynthia caught me in the kitchen later and tipped her chin toward Shortie. "Tell me about this guy."

"I will, but let's start the party first."

We played games, Chloe and Tom opened gifts, and we ate most of the food and cupcakes, CB sneaking a few licks. Lauree went home, and Chloe's friends left. Exhausted by the celebration, Chloe lay on the couch, her feet propped up, while Shortie, Hazel, and I helped load the presents into Tom's two-door sedan.

I tapped its roof. "You need a bigger vehicle."

He made a face and deadpanned, "Yes, Mother."

"I'm just saying. Gotta have room for my grandbaby."

Hazel waved her hand. "I have plenty of space in my Bug."

"Chloe does, too, in her car." Tom attempted to close his trunk but had to rearrange several of the gifts. He tried again, and it clicked shut. "It's not like I'll carry nine thousand baby items around."

He didn't understand it yet, but his world would change soon, in a big way. They may not need nine thousand baby belongings, but they would have a lot. We entered the house and found Carter, Mary, and Cynthia in a semi-circle around Chloe, chatting and laughing. The dog sat at Carter's feet and enjoyed a back scratch.

"Guess what, Mom?" Chloe called.

"Wait, let me tell her." Cynthia ran her hands through her hair.

"What's happening?" I asked.

She stood, balled her fists, and inhaled. She exhaled and, in a rush of words, said, "I left the Navy. I brought my stuff home, and I want to stay here." Her eyebrows raised, and her voice wavered. "If it's okay?"

A million questions flew through my mind. "Of course. Why didn't you tell me?"

"I've thought about it for a while. I just decided for sure. I had to either reenlist for another term or get out." She shrugged. "So, I got out."

"Is everything all right?" I asked, concerned she decided too quickly.

"Yes, Mom, I promise." She turned to her siblings. "Can y'all help me with my things? Wait, not you, Chloe." She gestured to the couch. "You lay there. Mary, can you help Carter and me?"

The trio carried Cynthia's assorted totes and suitcases inside and piled them in the middle of my living room.

Shortie eyed the mound. "We took at least as much to Tom's car."

"Yeah ..." Where would I put her and all her belongings?

Hazel stood and headed for the room she lived in for the last eight months. "Let me clear out of your room."

"No, Grandma," Cynthia said. "I can take the middle bedroom. You're all settled into my old one."

"Hazel?" I paused, not wanting to hurt her feelings. "Are you moving home now that your roof is fixed?"

Hazel toed the carpet. "Well, I wondered if I could stay. Sell my house and live here. With you." She looked at me, hope shining in her eyes.

Okay then. My nest was growing.

Chapter 2

Not quite a year ago, I owned and managed a thriving mom blog—Mamma Birds—but loneliness hit, and I formed the Empty Nesters Birding Group because of a reader's suggestion. One birder, Anna, died by accident, and another, Sylvia, was murdered. Stabbed, to be precise.

My mother-in-law moved in with me when Hurricane Hazel changed from a Category 1 storm to a nasty Cat 3 and headed straight for Pensacola. She didn't want to be alone during the hurricane, and she never left.

She and I bonded—a pair of widows connected by Zack, her son, and my deceased husband. Long story short, she joined me as my sidekick in the search for the killer.

In the back of my mind, I thought I would be an empty nester again once they fixed her roof and she returned home, taking her Weimaraner and parakeet. Carter would attend the University of South Alabama in Mobile. Chloe and Tom lived a short thirty-minute drive away in Gulf Breeze. And Cynthia would still be on active duty in the Navy.

Now, Cynthia and Hazel would live in two of my three extra bedrooms.

Carter waved his hand, a sheepish expression on his face. "Mom? Um, I plan to move back in a couple weeks. Finals ended, and my lease is almost up."

Oh, I forgot about that. Okay then. *All* of my bedrooms would be full.

I stood before my family, arms spread wide, my emotions soaring. "You guys are all welcome here, all the time. Any time. You're my people, and I love you. We'll make this work." I hugged them one by one.

Tom wiggled his eyebrows. "What if we want to move in?"

"It might be a bit tight, but you can if you have to." My mind raced as I rearranged rooms and determined who could sleep where.

Shortie winked. "I'm staying at my place."

"Good thing, buster, because I don't see a ring yet," Hazel chided him.

Uh-oh, time to change the subject. Fast. "Okay, anyone want pizza for dinner?" I picked up my cell and dialed the number. "How many pepperoni and mushroom, and how many deluxe?"

Shortie shook his head, lips turned up in a grin. We'd been dating seven months, at my count, and our relationship moved at a slow pace. I liked it and thought he did too. I cared about him, but neither of us had said the three little words, "I love you." Yet. As my first boyfriend since Zack died well over a decade ago, he wasn't a rebound boyfriend.

But I wanted to make sure it was real love. A lasting love.

Besides, now I had a houseful of kids, animals, and a mother-in-law to take care of, plus a grandbaby due soon. My hands itched to find a pen and paper and make a grocery list, and my brain whirred with all I had to do.

The Keatons, their return to Pensacola, and the Spanish caravel were put on the back burner.

I woke to the yummy aroma of bacon and coffee. After a long stretch and a jaw-popping yawn, I hopped out of bed and dressed. My walking boot sat in the corner of my room—a silent reminder of how close I came to dying last year. Thankful my ankle healed well, I slipped into sparkly red sandals and opened my bedroom door.

Cynthia stood at the stove and waved a spatula. "Morning, Mom."

I kissed her cheek and poured a cup of coffee. "Those eggs look yummy. And you made bacon. When did you start cooking?"

"I've been on a boat for four years. In my spare time, I cooked. I watched online videos to learn what to do, and—" She shrugged. "It's become a passion."

She dished out our breakfast, and we ate at the island. CB, hope in his eyes, waited for a bite.

"I let him out to potty this morning. Grandma wasn't up yet," she said.

"Thanks. He's a good fellow." I rubbed his back with my foot and then dropped him a piece of bacon.

"You're going to make him fat." Hazel's gruff voice startled me.

"He will never be fat. Weimaraners are sleek dogs. Right, CB?"

He woofed in agreement.

Cynthia stood and indicated her barstool. "Grandma, have a seat, and I'll dish your food."

Hazel scrutinized my plate. "She cooks? That'll be handy." She slid onto her seat.

True. I wasn't Julia Child, but I made the basics. Other than the one time Hazel made spaghetti—denying it was my last meal before I went to the police station to be fingerprinted—she had zero kitchen skills.

"What will you do since you've quit the Navy?" she asked.

Leave it to her to ask the difficult questions. I held my breath and waited for my daughter's answer.

She poured coffee for Hazel, filled her grandmother's plate, and set it down. "I thought about going to culinary school. I didn't quit. I needed to reenlist, and I decided not to."

What else affected her decision? She entered the Navy right after high school through the delayed entry program. She'd dreamed about doing that forever. "I thought you liked serving?"

She leaned against the island and tipped her head side to side. "I did."

"And?" Hazel asked.

"I loved being in the Navy. When we went to the North Atlantic—" Her expression grew wistful. "I enjoyed it. I liked my work as a yeoman. Sometimes. A lot of paperwork, though."

"Were you bored?" I topped off my coffee and returned to the barstool. "Restless?"

"Both, I guess. PSC has a culinary arts program, and I'm interested in trying it."

It took me a minute to translate PSC in my head. "I'm still not used to the name Pensacola State College. When I went, it was Pensacola Junior College."

She made a face. "You're old."

"Funny girl."

Cynthia rapped the counter with her knuckles. "Do y'all mind cleaning up? I'm going for a walk."

I waved my fork and mumbled around a mouthful of eggs, "Sure. Be careful."

Hazel helped clean the kitchen and left for the library. I

took my phone and laptop and headed for the back porch. CB followed me and stretched out in a patch of sunshine.

So far, May had been the epitome of a gorgeous spring with long, cool days, little humidity, lots of sunshine, and soft breezes. I enjoyed any time Pensacola had good weather. Not so hot and sticky, and my hair wasn't a frizzy, curly mess. Most of the year, I needed a lot of products to tame it.

I set my devices on a round wrought-iron table and curled up in a pale green Adirondack chair, a Christmas gift from Shortie. Its mate sat empty on the other side of the table, waiting for him to join me after work.

Several feeders hung from tall, skinny pine trees in my backyard. Red-winged blackbirds ate the suet from a square, flat feeder.

According to an old tale, red-winged blackbirds symbolize luck and protection. I didn't believe in luck, and God protected me, but I loved seeing them and all the other birds, squirrels, and occasional raccoons and bunnies that traipsed through the yard. CB didn't bark at the critters but closely observed their every move.

I closed my eyes and prayed. Last fall, I sat out here doing the same thing—mourning Carter leaving for college and that I was an empty nester. Now, I spent my time praising God for the new grandbaby to come and for my kids' health and happiness. And that I would have more time with Cynthia and Carter.

My phone rang, startling me from my prayers. I hit accept and the speaker button.

"Hey, lady."

My pulse ramped up at Shortie's husky voice. "Hi. How's your day?"

"Busy. These young guys, whew. I hope I wasn't so incompetent when I joined the Navy." After serving for over twenty years as an MP, Shortie now worked as a contractor at Naval Air Station (NAS) Pensacola.

"You've never been incompetent."

"Thanks." He paused. "I wanted to talk to you about something. Can I take you to dinner Sunday night?"

My stomach flipped at his serious tone. "Um, sure."

"Don't sound too excited, Peg."

"No, I am, promise. I thought I'd schedule a birding trip out to Fort Pickens. How's that sound?"

"Like fun. This Saturday?" he said.

"Yes, if everyone can make it. I'll text them and let you know."

"Okay, talk to you later." He blew me a kiss and ended the call.

I set my phone aside and wondered what he wanted to discuss. It might be bad news or good news. I tended to be pessimistic and think the worst.

I looked up. "You got this, right? I'll wait on You." I would repeat the words over and over until Sunday's dinner date. I found it challenging to pursue my own happiness, especially with Shortie. Several months ago, Hazel asked me to dream about what I wanted at this stage in my life, and it wasn't only romance I struggled with.

From comments on my Mamma Birds blog, I realized many moms felt guilty about wanting a life apart from their kids. I encouraged them and said it wasn't a bad thing. In fact, it was healthy. Why wouldn't I do the same for myself? My kids didn't require me to be "on deck" at all times. They weren't kids anymore. They were grownups. I'd done my job. They might need me occasionally, but I didn't have to wait around for them.

My thoughts were interrupted when Cynthia joined me.

"Hey, Mom." She plopped in the other chair, sweat trickling down her cheeks. She patted CB's head.

"Good walk?"

"More of a fast one, so I'm hot and sweaty." She wiped her face with a hand towel. "Much better now than in August, though."

"True. What are you up to today?"

"After I shower, I'm heading to PSC to apply and see if I can enroll in some summer classes. How about you?"

"I need to work on the blog a bit. Carter called, and he'll be home two weeks from yesterday, so I want to clean his room. And I'm going to text the birding group to arrange our next outing."

Cynthia stopped mid-wipe, eyebrow cocked. "I've heard all about the birders. Sounds like a dangerous group."

I chuckled at the thought of mild-mannered retired history professor Owen and the somewhat ostentatious realtor, Carmen, bearing weapons and looking fierce.

"They're not dangerous. Right now, it's me, Grandma, Shortie, Owen, and Carmen."

"Two people died last year. Like right off the bat."

Someone, Hazel or Chloe, had filled the child's ear. "There's a bit more to the story. Shortie played a big part in catching the killer. Wanna hear it?"

I told the tale, and she listened, most of the time with her mouth hanging open.

"I discovered Sylvia, the murdered birder," I said. "Then her killer pushed me down a flight of steep stairs, and I ended up with a broken ankle, and the killer tied up Grandma. Shortie saved the day by catching the bad guy." I didn't offer the new information on Roger and Estelle.

I finished, and she shook her head and stood. "Next birding trip, I'm going too."

"Why?"

"Someone's gotta keep an eye on y'all." She headed inside, muttering about crazy old people and killers.

Hmm. The tables had turned. I caused my kid anxiety. I snickered at the thought.

I opened my laptop and navigated to my blog, Mamma Birds. Lauree now carried the weight of blogging and took care of the business end of things. Chloe planned to start a section for new moms after the baby's birth. I covered what it was like to be an empty nester. Being a mom didn't stop when your kids grew up.

Now, I'd experience them at home as adults. I jotted a note to blog about the subject, sure I wasn't alone in this new phase.

Before writing, I texted Owen and Carmen about meeting at Fort Pickens on Pensacola Beach and received a "Yes" back from both. I texted Shortie to confirm 10 a.m. on Saturday. He responded with a thumbs-up emoji and a text.

No dead bodies this time, okay?

Like I intended to find dead people. I shot back the same emoji and shook my head. Last year brought enough bodies and killers. I wasn't interested in discovering more.

Chapter 3

Saturday morning, Cynthia was dressed and ready to accompany Hazel and me on our birding trip.

"I want to check out these people," she said. "Too many weird things have happened." She flexed her biceps. "I can be your protection."

Her fierceness made me giggle, but not out loud.

On the drive, we discussed how the Keatons sneaked back into Pensacola.

"It's amazing they did it. I can't believe either of them would have the guts to return," Hazel said, her lip curled.

"Explain to me their relationship to the murders last year," Cynthia said.

"The killer, Pensacola's mayor at the time, told Grandma how Estelle Keaton controlled the whole thing." I took the exit from Interstate 10 to I-110.

"You two are dangerous." In my rearview mirror, I saw Cynthia, arms crossed and shaking her head.

She had no idea.

I drove through Gulf Breeze, turned right at the colorful

sailfish Pensacola Beach sign, and used my prepaid pass to zip on through the unmanned toll booth to the beach.

"Well, they may think it all died down, but the Pensacola police are on the search for both of them. Estelle, at least, is still a suspect." I flipped on my turn signal to head right onto Fort Pickens Road.

"The mastermind." Hazel curled her fingers like a witch and cackled. "Maybe they were involved with the missing quetzal. Last year, they were in Guatemala, and the news said a quetzal went missing from one of the zoos."

"I wouldn't put it past them. Shortie told me not to investigate."

She wiggled her eyebrows. "We have no choice but to look into this."

Cynthia heaved a noisy sigh.

We drove past the Pensacola Beach cross, my favorite spot. CB and I visited it months ago while we were embroiled in the murder investigation. I opened the windows and inhaled the scents of the Gulf, the sand, and the road tar. Sand dunes, some larger than others, blocked my view of the water. Sea oats waved in a gentle breeze. And crying gulls raced my car. I paid the entrance fee to the park and drove to the Visitor's Center parking lot.

"There's Owen and Carmen." I waved.

Hazel narrowed her eyes. "Do you think she's interested in him? They always ride together."

I elbowed her, turned off the car, and unbuckled. "Come on. She's too young for him. You, though, are the right age."

She gave me the stink-eye.

Cynthia climbed out of my SUV and hooked her arm through her grandmother's. "You are prettier, too, Grandma. And smarter."

Hazel patted her hand. "You're my favorite."

Cynthia eyed me, and we broke into giggles.

Owen wore a tan sunhat on his head, strings tied in a knot under his chin.

"He's prepared," Hazel said.

"Always. That's what makes him Owen."

We joined them and entered the building. Shortie hustled in a few minutes later.

"Sorry, I'm late. I overslept." He shoved his fingers through his still-damp hair.

I stood on my tiptoes and kissed his cheek. "I'm glad you're here."

Hazel snapped open a brochure and read aloud, "It took over five years to build the fort."

"It served as a Union stronghold during the Civil War," Owen added. He puffed out his chest and surveyed our group over his reading glasses. "I am a retired history professor, remember?"

Mild-mannered, gentle Owen didn't often talk about his former job, teaching at the University of West Florida, but he still carried a professorial air about him.

Shortie picked up another brochure and flipped through it. "Aren't you a Civil War buff?"

Owen beamed, his smile as bright as the overhead lights gleaming on his bald head. "Yes, I am, and this place in particular, with all of its history. They built Pickens after the War of 1812 to fortify the area and protect the bay and the Navy yard. In 1861, the Confederates attacked the fort, but the Union defended it."

"Didn't Geronimo stay here?" I asked.

"Yes, as a prisoner." He shifted his feet and stood with his hands linked behind his back. "Geronimo was an Apache war chief and a medicine man. When the Apaches were forced onto reservations, he and his followers escaped and spent years raiding and killing. After his capture in 1886, some Pensacola business leaders arranged for him to be sent here. They 'claimed' he would be guarded better." He made air quotes around the word *claimed*.

"It didn't work out like they said? Did he die at the fort?" I slipped my hand into Shortie's, looking forward to spending the day with him.

"No, no. They put him and his band of men to work. Plus, he became a spectacle. One book I read indicated that an average of twenty visitors a day came to see him during his captivity. He ended up as a tourist attraction."

Carmen stepped back and covered her mouth. "How awful. Poor man."

Owen wiggled his hands back and forth. "Yes and no. They took advantage of him, true. He rode in President Teddy Roosevelt's inaugural parade and visited the World's Fair in St. Louis. But we can't forget he led raids and killed people. He died in Oklahoma in 1909."

"Where did they keep him here?" Cynthia asked.

"Good question, young lady." Owen waved toward the Visitor's Center exit. "Follow me, and I'll explain. We can bird-watch after."

Hazel walked beside him as we traipsed outside. He paused at the fort's entrance and began our history lesson with a gesture at the brick archway. "This is the sally port. It's the main entrance. Once, there were large oak doors and a wooden bridge leading to them." He pointed to the pavement under our feet.

We followed him into the officers' quarters. The interior walls, plaster-lined and chipped to expose the brick underneath, made it much cooler inside.

Hazel patted Owen's arm. "How many bricks are in here?"

She'd read the brochure, so she knew. I admired her blatant

attempt at flirting and tried to catch her eye, but she ignored me.

Carmen spoke up. "Over twenty-one million bricks. It said it in the flyer."

Owen nodded at her answer. "She's right. Geronimo's housing was believed to be located here on the south wall. The prisoners were guarded, and although over the years rumors said Geronimo had a private cell, I don't think this was true."

Hazel's shoulders slumped at his dismissal. Cynthia joined Shortie and me, and we explored the area, wandering a few feet from the rest of our group. She peeked around a corner into another dimmer part of the quarters and stepped inside.

"Mom, check this out." She called me over and held out a long, iridescent green feather.

"Owen can tell us what this belongs to." I called his name. "What is this?"

Shortie chuckled. "It's a bird feather. I could have told you."

I elbowed him. "Smart man. Yes, but what kind?"

Owen removed a bird book from his vest and thumbed through it. Hazel peered over his shoulder. He turned the book toward us. "Hmm, okay, I think it's this one."

She gasped. "It's a quetzal tail feather."

"You're right." Owen read for a minute. "This says that in ancient Mayan culture, the Mayans used quetzal feathers as a kind of money because quetzals were considered sacred."

Shortie, Hazel, Cynthia, and I exchanged glances.

Carmen joined us. "Why are you looking at each other like that?" Her finely tweezed eyebrows crinkled, and she hooked her arm through Owen's. "Let's continue the tour."

"I haven't told you two, but the Keatons are back in Pensacola. Last year, they were in Guatemala, and a quetzal went missing," I said.

Owen barked a dismissive laugh. "You think this feather is from the missing quetzal? That's quite a stretch, Peg."

"Maybe, but quetzals don't live in the United States."

Cynthia tugged my shirt sleeve. "Mom?"

I turned at the fear in her voice. "What's wrong?" I scanned her head to toe, alert for any problems.

She pointed. Several feet from where she found the feather was a pile of leaves with something—it looked like a black sneaker—poking out of them.

"Huh? Weird. Where did the leaves come from? There aren't any trees outside this part of the fort," I said.

Hazel stepped farther into the room and leaned down, brushing away more of the leaves. The shoe was connected to a leg, and she screamed.

"Why are you here?" I asked. The man in front of me wore a dark brown button-down shirt and blue jeans. He rolled up the sleeves on his tanned, muscled forearms. I dragged my gaze from the sight.

"Nice to see you again, Peg." Marcus Sharp's sarcasm rang loud and clear. He shook Shortie's hand. "They called me in because of the Keatons and their link to Sylvia Newman and Anna Thompson's murders."

I met Detective Sharp last September at the birding group's first outing when Anna died from anaphylactic shock after she handled birdseed laced with peanuts. The peanuts, intended to kill Sylvia, resulted in Anna's accidental death.

I reminded myself not to stare. When we first met, his dimples and dark brown eyes, the same shade as his shirt, attracted me. It didn't take long before a harder and more competitive side of him showed and discouraged any further relationship. He apologized, but we weren't friends anymore.

Now, we watched as EMTs loaded Roger Keaton's body into the coroner's van. I sighed. Another death, another murder.

Shortie introduced Marcus to Cynthia, who stayed glued to my side. Sharp acknowledged her with a nod and pulled a notebook from his pocket. He flipped it open. "What can you tell me?"

"You'll be surprised to hear this, but I didn't discover Keaton." I clenched my fists, my fingernails pressed into my palms.

"You didn't?" His words dripped more sarcasm. He turned to Shortie. "You?"

"Nope, not me. Hazel found him." He called my mother-in-law over.

She rushed to us, shielding her eyes with her hand. "I can tell you everything, Marcus. I was about to talk to those park rangers." She pointed to the group clustered nearby. Their cowboy-hat-style straw hats, tan uniform shirts, and sharply pressed olive pants indicated their identity.

He cringed. "Hazel, please call me Detective Sharp."

"You can call me Mrs. Howard." She popped her hands on her hips, her blue eyes blazing. "You want to hear what I found or not? Why aren't you in uniform? You were the last time we saw you."

Sharp's face flushed. He nodded and spoke through gritted teeth. "Detectives don't wear uniforms. When you met me then, I had just become a detective and hadn't switched over. Now, please tell me what you found."

Hazel explained Cynthia's discovery of the sneaker and how she herself found the body attached to it—Keaton's body. "I brushed off some leaves from him. I didn't turn or touch him. He lay face up, and we identified him right away. He had a bullet hole in the middle of his forehead but no blood. Why wasn't there any blood?"

Marcus scribbled notes. "Thanks. I'll be in touch if I have more questions. You still live with Peg?" His gaze held mine.

"Yes, I do," Hazel said.

He slapped shut his notebook and marched off to join the national park rangers.

Shortie indicated the uniformed men and women. "They'll handle most of this, but Sharp has to figure out how Keaton got out here. And who killed him."

Hazel's mouth twisted to one side. "I want to know why there wasn't blood by Roger's body."

"I don't want to see any, but thanks. I wonder how long he's been out here." I blew out a long breath. "Do you think his wife killed him?"

Hazel gasped. "I bet she did. I'll go tell Marcus."

Shortie grasped her arm before she followed after the detective. "Hold on. He's aware Estelle is in Pensacola. It was on the news."

"Oh, yeah." She covered her face with her hands and released a deep sigh.

I slung an arm around her waist. "Let's round up the rest of the birders and go find some birds." I leaned closer to her ear and whispered, "We'll talk about this at home."

She perked up and mimed zipping her lips closed.

Our group remained subdued, but with Owen again leading the way, we hiked around the area and spotted several different kinds of birds—tiny warblers, orioles, and brown pelicans. The sun warmed us, and the breeze off the Gulf kept us comfortable. A brick retaining wall separated the road from the beach. We walked up and over several steps and tromped through the soft white sand to the shoreline.

Across Pensacola Bay, part of the sunken caravel stuck above the water. I pointed it out to Hazel.

"I wonder what kind of treasures they'll find," she said.

"Gold, silver, and gems, like the rumors say?"

Her eyes twinkled. "How exciting! It's more interesting than the artifacts they've found from the de Luna wrecks. Weapons, plates, and nails aren't as fun as gems."

Cynthia touched my arm and gestured to a pelican. "Look at him dive." She grinned and imitated his motion with her arm.

Her smile lightened my heart.

The bird plunged into the Gulf again, and Owen cracked open his book. "Brown pelicans are small, and unlike other pelicans, they plunge for their food.

A smallish bird with a yellow bill and legs and what resembled a black helmet caught my eye. As I watched, it took flight.

"What's that?" I asked.

Carmen stepped forward and spoke, "I can identify it. It's a least tern."

We all turned to stare at her.

"Have you been researching birds?" Hazel asked, her brows furrowed and one eyebrow cocked.

Carmen studied her nails and made a face. "Kind of. I wanted to contribute to the group. I'm not the typical birder type."

She told the truth. Most of us wore shorts—Owen, Cynthia, and Shortie sported the khaki cargo kind—an old T-shirt, and hiking boots. Carmen wore color-coordinated clothes: white capris with a dressy red, white, and blue top, red sandals, and a scarf tied around her neck.

Hazel mumbled, "Trying to impress Owen is what she's doing."

I held my finger to my lips. "Shush." Louder, I said, "I'm impressed, Carmen. What other terns have you learned about?"

She stood straight and delivered a lecture on the different terns in Northwest Florida. Hazel might have reason to worry about Carmen and Owen, but I loved seeing birder-Carmen, not the real estate agent persona she usually portrayed.

I led a round of clapping when she finished speaking. "You've learned a lot."

"Thank you." A blush worked its way up her neck.

I opened my mouth to ask her another question when Cynthia grabbed my arm and said, "Mom, look."

Chapter 4

A bright blue tarp, large enough to wrap a body in, lay tucked into scrub brush several yards to our left. Patches of darker areas showed, and as I stepped closer, I realized they were blood, with more of it in the sand and surrounding dirt.

The rest of the group crowded around me.

Hazel gripped my arm, her nails digging into my forearm. "Is that what I think it is?"

Shortie squatted and picked up a small stick. He pushed aside some debris and examined the ground. I stepped toward the brush.

"Don't touch it." He gestured to the dirt. "It must be from Roger." He joined me and peered at the tarp.

"Mom?" Cynthia's voice quavered.

I waved her to my side. "I know this is scary, honey. We need to tell the police officer what we've found."

She drew a deep breath and straightened up, fists clenched. "I can find him," she said, nodding as if to reassure herself.

Carmen raised a trembling hand, her face pale. "I'll go with her."

"Owen, can you accompany them?" Shortie asked. "I don't want the women alone."

My lips twitched. If it came to it, Cynthia could defend herself, Carmen, and Owen. Cynthia raised her eyebrows but kept her mouth shut.

They rounded the corner in search of Marcus, and I bit back a sigh, anticipating his reaction. The first time I met him, he was calm and had his notebook at the ready, his constant companion. He might still be organized, but his composure, at least with me, had flown the coop. Every time we were together, we both became frustrated and irritated, often over dead bodies. Something else floated between us. I pushed the thought to the back of my mind.

"What in the world is going on? How did we, of all people, find another dead body *and* a bloody tarp?" Hazel said.

I laughed at her incredulous tone. "You found this one. Not me."

Shortie stood to the side, glancing from the tarp to the water's edge. He pointed. "You can tell where someone dragged it." He walked the track, staying far enough away to keep from disturbing the area.

The soft sand at the water's edge showed more of a dip. As the track reached the harder dirt and sand combination, the ground became firmer and the indention almost disappeared. I pictured a body wrapped in the fabric and towed through the sand. I shuddered.

"You think the tarp held Keaton?" Hazel's eyes gleamed. "He would weigh it down and show better in the sand, wouldn't he?"

"I think so. They'll have to test the blood." He joined us and examined the tarp again, his forehead wrinkled. "Lot of it on this."

"Do. Not. Touch. That."

Marcus Sharp had arrived. He struggled walking in the sand, waddling side to side. I stifled a smirk.

Shortie stepped back, hands up. "I didn't, man. See the track here? You can tell where someone dragged the tarp. Peg found blood on the ground too." He waved from the scrub brush to the water.

"We think it held Roger Keaton's body." Hazel bounced on her toes and rubbed her hands together. "Another murder to solve."

Marcus glared at her. She hung her head and came to stand beside me.

"He's no fun," she whispered.

"We don't need your birding group out here messing up the area, Peg." The detective's nostrils flared, his eyes cold and hard. The way he said, 'birding group,' raised my hackles.

"I stayed a good foot away from the tarp and the track." Shortie scowled. "You do remember I used to be a cop."

Marcus huffed.

"We are leaving anyhow. You're welcome for finding this and telling you. I'm sure it makes your job easier." I hooked my arms through Cynthia's and Hazel's and stalked off, the other birders tromping behind me.

We grumbled and muttered our way to the parking lot. Owen was annoyed because our bird-watching had been cut short. Hazel expressed irritation over how Marcus commandeered the situation, and Carmen whined about her feet hurting.

Shortie pulled me aside before I reached my car. "I don't want to go to lunch today. I'll see you tomorrow evening, okay?"

I palmed my forehead. "Oh, yeah. Sure."

He shook his head, lips twitching. "I love how excited you are to spend time with me."

I stood on my tiptoes for a kiss. "I am. Always. But this murder thing." I shrugged. "You know how I am."

"I do." He winked.

My stomach flipped. Those words and the affection in his eyes made me wonder once more about what he wanted to discuss on our date.

"Remember what I said, though. You stay out of it." He tapped my nose.

Hmm, way to throw cold water on my plans.

He hugged me and left. Owen and Carmen drove off without a word, so I assumed they didn't want lunch either.

I joined Hazel and Cynthia by my car. "Anyone hungry? Everyone else left."

They both shook their heads. We were a lot quieter heading home than when our day started.

ON SUNDAY AFTERNOON, I cleaned Carter's room and ran the vacuum throughout the house. Then I stopped to dress for my date. I showered and took my time with my hair and applying mascara and lipstick. I slipped into a soft, flowy blue sundress. Who knew how this evening would go? I wanted to be prepared.

Shortie knocked at seven sharp, and he whistled when he saw me. "You look amazing." He spun his finger, and I twirled for him. "Beautiful inside and out."

"You clean up pretty good yourself."

His broad shoulders and muscled arms stretched the sleeves of his dark gray polo. He offered his arm. "Let's go. We have lots to talk about."

The butterflies in my stomach went on high alert. I trusted him and wanted to open up more. Then, nerves took over, and

I chattered about meaningless stuff the whole way to our favorite seafood restaurant on Pensacola Beach.

He parked and shifted to face me. "You done?"

I closed my eyes, heat rising up my neck into my face. "Sorry."

"Peg, don't worry. We'll have a nice evening." He squeezed my hand.

I opened my eyes and looked into his gray ones.

"You trust me, right?"

"Yes." The word came out in a whisper.

He turned off the car, came to my side, opened the door, and held out his hand. I felt like the princess did when she met the street rat. Except Shortie wasn't a ruffian. A strong, faithful man, he showed his commitment to me and my family. I loved spending time with him, but I held back in our relationship, and I didn't know why. When Hazel helped me explore my dreams, I realized I loved to write, blog, and help people. We never discussed my romantic plans, which would have been a bit embarrassing with my mother-in-law.

Too bad I hadn't talked to Lauree before this important date.

I took his hand and followed him up the weathered steps of the building and inside the restaurant. Shortie requested a table in the corner and ordered Oysters Rockefeller. The waitress brought them along with two sweet teas and took our orders. I chose chargrilled fresh grouper—my mouth watered thinking about it. Shortie debated ordering grilled shrimp or red beans and rice. He picked the shrimp, closed his menu, and handed it to the waitress.

He reached for a small plate and dished three oysters for each of us. Baked with spinach, parmesan cheese, and bacon, they were our favorite appetizer. My stomach rumbled in happy anticipation.

I ate one and closed my eyes. "These are so yummy." I opened my eyes and saw a folded magazine lying on the table. "What is this?"

He tapped it with one finger. "It's what I wanted to talk to you about."

I leaned in. The magazine had all kinds of car ads—old cars, classic cars, and junkers. I burst out laughing. I worried all this time about a magazine with old jalopies for sale.

His brows drew together in a frown. "What's so funny?"

I popped another oyster in my mouth and mumbled around my food. "Oh, nothing. It's all good." I wasn't sharing all of my crazy thoughts. "So, what is this?"

He settled back in his seat and started talking. The more I learned about Shortie, the more I realized I didn't know about him. According to his tale, he loved to work on old cars as a kid. He intended to buy one, fix it up, and resell it.

"I wanted to run the idea past you. See what you think." He sipped his tea and waited for my answer.

The waitress approached with our food. I leaned back, and she set our orders in front of us.

"Y'all need anything else?" she asked.

We both shook our heads, and I turned back to Shortie.

"Well, I am surprised. I did not know you were a gearhead."

His lips tipped up in a grin, and he shrugged. "Always have been, but I didn't have time for it in the Navy. Now I do."

"I say, if you want to do it, go for it. What's stopping you?" I ate my last oyster, set my appetizer plate aside, and moved on to the grouper.

"It's a risk."

I pointed my fork at him. "You don't strike me as someone afraid of taking a chance."

"True." He picked up a shrimp and studied it. "If I were a risk-taker, I would have gotten crawfish."

"Mudbugs," I said through another bite of fish. "They're nasty." I wrinkled my nose.

"I agree. That's why we make such a good team."

After dinner, we walked across Fort Pickens Road to the beach. The moon glowed on the ocean, offering plenty of light for a romantic stroll. A soft breeze played in my curls. I took an appreciative sniff of the salt and sand combination—one of my favorites.

But Shortie's focus? Cars, cars, cars.

He kicked off his shoes and left them at the top of the beach. "I thought I might start with old Chevys. A Camaro, if I can find an inexpensive one." He followed me to the water's edge, chattering about his plans.

"It's an old car. How expensive is it? A couple hundred?" I slipped off my sandals and let the water splash on my feet.

Shortie snorted. "More like several thousand?" He shook his head and pulled me to a stop. He ran his thumb down my cheek and over my lips.

I closed my eyes, anticipating his kiss.

"Here's the thing," he said. "If I do this, it'll take more of my time."

My eyes shot open. "What?"

"This would be a side job for me. I won't be able to come over as often." He tucked his hands in his pockets, his mouth pulled into a grimace.

"Oh," I whispered. Here, I thought he wanted to take the next step in our relationship. Not marriage, but a ring or a promise. "I see."

I turned and headed back up the sand toward the road.

"Where are you going?"

"I'm ready to go home," I called over my shoulder. I

couldn't tell him how I felt because I wasn't sure. So, I hadn't said those three little words yet. Neither had he. And what he'd said tonight told me he wouldn't.

I may be slow on the uptake, but I'm not stupid.

He joined me as I slipped on my sandals and pulled me in for a hug. "I didn't mean to hurt your feelings." He leaned back and wiped tears from my face. "Why are you crying?"

I shook my head and shrugged, more tears falling. I swiped them away with my fingertips, surprised at how upset I felt. "It's okay, I'm tired."

Worry filled his eyes. "I think it's more than that."

It was, but I wasn't telling him. I needed time alone to think about what he said and what he hadn't said. A black sedan whizzed by as I stepped onto the road to cross over to the parking lot. I caught a flash of an orange license plate.

Shortie pulled me back against his body. "What are you doing? Be careful." Tension filled his voice.

"I didn't even hear it." I tipped my head. Black sedan, dark tinted windows. "Huh. That car looked like Estelle Keaton's. The license plate was orange. Think we can catch up with it?"

Shortie closed his eyes and sighed. He held out his hand. "I'm enabling you, but come on."

This was the man I knew.

Chapter 5

I buckled up, and Shortie jammed the Jeep into gear and took off. I leaned forward and searched for the car. It wasn't anywhere we passed.

"Can you go faster?"

"I'll enable, but I don't want a ticket."

I swallowed a groan. "We won't find them. It's too dark, and they had too much of a head start." I pointed to the central parking lot on the beach. "Let's drive through here just in case."

We drove end to end. I peeked inside all the black cars and walked around them to check license plates—no orange woman veteran ones with a BRDS ALIV plate. When I finished, Shortie parked under the Pensacola Beach water tower and turned to me.

"Other than driving up and down the beach for hours chasing a car that might not be Estelle Keaton's, do you want to go for a walk or go home?"

Easy answer. "I want to go home." I sat back, arms crossed, and stewed. He might not think it was Keaton's car, but I did. I needed to see that license plate—a distinctive, personalized one. Assuming she hadn't replaced it, it should be easy to identify. If it was Estelle's car, she might have hidden evidence at the fort. Why else would she have come from that direction?

Shortie headed toward Pensacola, crossed the bridge, and took I-110. After driving several minutes, he blurted, "Tell me what's wrong. I can't read your mind."

His words startled me out of my funk. He sat with his shoulders hunched, hands clenching the steering wheel, and his jaw muscle twitching.

"I'm fine. I was thinking about the Keatons."

He looked at me and blinked. "You were?"

"Yeah." I explained my thoughts about what Estelle might be up to.

"What happened on the beach? Between you and me?"

Oh. What to say now? I had already shifted to worrying about Estelle Keaton. Shortie's words took me back to our earlier interaction. The date hadn't gone like I thought it would. And I wasn't ready to talk about it.

He shook his head. "You pulled away."

I swallowed and managed to choke on my spit. I hacked and coughed until he handed me a spare water bottle from the cubby in his door.

"Thanks." I cleared my throat. "Whew. Sorry."

"So?" He stopped at a red light, his eyes filled with worry, and his lips pulled into the saddest frown.

I fiddled with the water bottle cap. "The car thing surprised me."

The light turned green. He steered into the turning lane to take me home. "That's all?"

"Yep." I took another sip.

And that's how our wonderful, special evening ended.

In the famous chubby pig's words—*That's all, folks.*

MONDAY DAWNED BRIGHT AND SUNNY—ANOTHER beautiful late spring day in northwest Florida. I shuffled to the coffeepot, still in my nightshirt, which was covered in sleeping dogs, and said, "Ready for a nap." The perfect shirt for this day.

I slumped on the couch and sipped my java, then clicked on the television and tuned into the local news.

"Blah, blah, blah." A news story about the caravel caught my attention. It switched to a live report out at Fort Pickens. I was so caught up in getting ready for my date on Sunday that I forgot to check for new information on Roger's death. Or murder. This story might reveal more news and tell if Estelle had been found.

"Roger Keaton's body was discovered Saturday here inside Fort Pickens." The newsperson gestured to the structure behind her. Her long, blonde hair blew across her face, and she spit out a strand. "Oops, sorry."

I rolled my eyes.

"Some tourists found the body under a pile of leaves. Park Rangers were called, followed by Pensacola Detective Marcus Sharp."

A clip of Marcus discussing the previous year's murder and its relationship to Roger and Estelle Keaton followed. I sat back and watched his dark eyes. My fingers tingled, remembering how it felt to trace his dimple.

"Ugh." I clicked off the TV and shook my head. "I need to get a life." Seeing Marcus, not to mention the reporter, irritated me.

Hazel and CB entered the room. "You okay?" she asked. CB wagged his tail.

"Fine." I pushed myself off the couch. "I'm getting more coffee. You want some?"

"Sure. How did your date go?" She sat at the island.

"It was okay." I handed her a mug filled to the brim. "Here."

We drank our coffee in silence. Hazel perched on a barstool while I leaned against the kitchen counter. I finished my second cup, poured a third, and offered her more.

She shook her head. "You're very quiet." Her words were laced with concern, but curiosity filled her eyes.

I grunted. "I'm going back to bed." I shuffled to my room and closed the door. "Ugh." Disgust filled me. Moody over a boy. "I'm not in middle school." I changed into my swimsuit and found a pool towel and my goggles.

"Hazel? Cynthia?" No one answered, so I left them a note. A long swim at the University of West Florida pool should cheer me up. Or at least work off some of my irritation. If not, I would stop on the way home and buy a kitchen sink cookie. Thinking of the yummy cookie full of chocolate chips, pecans, caramel, and more cheered me up—a little.

When I started the Empty Nesters Birding Group, Lauree and I created a flyer and hung it on the UWF clubhouse bulletin board. I avoided looking for it when I went to the women's locker room. I was on a mission. I stuffed my bathing suit coverup, keys, and wallet into a locker, rinsed off in the shower, and headed for the pool. This time of year, it ran the entire length instead of the width. I picked a lane and dove in. I didn't want to talk to anyone or even make eye contact. I swam until my arms hung limp, and my lungs screamed.

I pulled myself out, untangled my goggles from my curls, toweled off, and retrieved my things. The swim helped, but a cookie still sounded inviting. I walked by the bulletin board and noticed the flyer had a few tear-offs with my phone number left. A slim, handsome man about my age stood in front of it.

I stopped and gestured to the piece of paper. "I hung this

flyer for the birding group. Are you interested? Do you have any questions?"

He pulled off his glasses and chewed on the stem. I held back a smile. At second glance, he looked more like a grad student attempting to appear professorial than someone my age.

I stuck out my hand. "Peg Howard, reckless leader of the Empty Nesters Birding Group. You don't look old enough to have kids, let alone grownup ones, but anyone is welcome in our nest." I grinned at my clever play on words.

He regarded me for a moment before one corner of his mouth turned up, and he shook my hand. "Let's just say I'm older than I appear, shall we? Dr. Harry Morrison, ma'am."

I gestured to the board, resisting the urge to ask to see his driver's license, "We haven't scheduled our next outing, but I will soon." No way would I mention Roger Keaton's dead body. Or Sylvia's. Or Anna's.

Boy, the body count had built up.

I grabbed one of the tear-offs with my number and held it out to him. "Here. Give me a call this week if you want to join us. There are just a few in our group. You may know one— Owen Walters. He used to teach history here on campus."

His gaze held mine as he reached for the paper. Our fingers touched, a zing zapping me clear to my toes. "Thanks, Peg. I'll be calling."

Wow. I had never been a sucker for hazel eyes and glasses. Maybe it was time for me to try something new.

Dr. Harry and Shortie filled my thoughts all the way home. Shortie and I weren't over, but I wasn't sure where we stood. What was so easy and long-term a couple of days ago now was like a wooden bridge swinging over a deep drop-off. Depending on which way either of us moved, our future would be on firm ground or over in an instant.

I huffed, irritated that I still had men on my mind. What was wrong with me? I forgot about my cookie until the garage door closed behind my car.

Cynthia sat at the island, twirling the quetzal feather in her hands.

"How was the swim?" she asked.

I made a face. "Okay."

Hazel entered the room, stopped, and put her hands on her hips. "*Okay. Fine.* That's all I've gotten out of her today." She stepped closer and peered into my eyes, then waved a hand in front of my face. CB sat at my feet and contributed his opinion with a bark.

I glared at her and the dog. "If you must know, I met a man at the pool." Cynthia and Hazel gaped at me. The dog did, too, although he may have been panting. While they were occupied, I poured myself a glass of water and chugged it down, using my pool towel to wipe my mouth. I plopped the glass on the counter. "I'm going to shower and wash off the chlorine."

Hazel called out, "We'll be here when you're done."

True to her word, she and Cynthia sat perched on the barstools when I came out of my room. I towel-dried my hair, scrunching and finger-combing it into place. "Y'all are patient."

"Not really." Hazel tapped her fingers on the counter.

"What are you up to, Mom?" Cynthia chimed in at the same time.

I tossed my towel in the laundry room and made a mental note to run the wash soon. Taking a deep breath, I let it out slowly. "I am fine." I held a hand up to stave off Hazel's words.

"Shortie and I, well, our date was … disappointing. I thought we were more serious than we are." I shrugged, attempting to portray indifference and ignoring the emotion building behind my eyes.

Hazel blinked. "I thought things were going very well. Like possibly marriage well."

I grimaced, and my eye twitched. *Me too.*

Cynthia stood and hugged me. "As long as you're okay." She leaned back. "I can beat him up if you want me to."

"Funny girl. No, no. We're still seeing each other." At least, I thought so.

"You met a man at the pool?" Hazel propped her chin in her palm and fluttered her eyelashes. "Tell all."

"He was reading the flyer for the birding group. I didn't tell him about Roger, but I told him to call me if he wanted to join us. I think he's a grad student."

She perked up. "A younger man. Ooh. Describe him. What does he do?"

"I didn't ask him. He introduced himself as Dr. Harry Morrison." I popped two pieces of bread into the toaster and got the butter and marmalade from the refrigerator. "So, he's not a grad student. I doubt he'll call. He was probably just being polite."

My cell rang as I finished speaking. Hazel and Cynthia peeked at the number.

Hazel's brows drew together, her eyes dark with worry. "It says unknown. Should you answer it?"

Cynthia picked up my phone and punched in the numbers to unlock it. "Why wouldn't she?" She held it out to me.

Hazel and I exchanged glances. I told Cynthia about Anna and Sylvia dying but never mentioned the anonymous phone calls. They all came from an unknown number, and last year's killer identified Estelle Keaton as the voice on the other end.

When I didn't take the device, Cynthia punched accept and speaker and set it down.

"Hello?" said a male voice.

Hazel and I blew out a breath at the same time. The knots in my stomach relaxed. I took my cell. "Hi, who is this?"

"Ms. Howard? This is Dr. Morrison. Um, Harry."

My automatic correction of "Mrs. Howard" didn't come out. Instead, I said, "Hi, Harry. I'm glad you called."

Chapter 6

"I wondered if you would schedule a birding trip soon. I'm in town for a few weeks." Adrenaline rushed through me at his modulated voice, nothing like Shortie's husky one.

"Of course I can. Are you a regular birder?" Heat climbed my neck. "I ... I mean, have you birded before?" Birded? Was that a verb? I smacked my forehead with my palm.

He laughed. "I should have given you a card. My Ph.D. is in wildlife with a specialty in ornithology. In other words, I study birds."

I closed my eyes. I asked this man who studied birds for a living if he'd ever been bird-watching. "Okay. I will schedule an outing. Can I text you at this number?"

"Yes, please do. And Peg? Can I call you Peg?"

"Yes." I avoided eye contact with Hazel and Cynthia.

"Well, Peg, I'm glad I ran into you today. I'll see you soon."

He hung up, and I whispered, "Me too."

Cynthia held up her fist. "Way to go, Mom. You're on fire."

Was she kidding me? I insulted the man, a professional, an expert in the field. I wasn't sure our raggedy band of birders would be up his alley. I returned her fist bump without enthusiasm. "I'm not sure you're right. I sounded like a simpleton."

Cynthia took her seat at the island. "No one says simpleton anymore." Her giggles were contagious.

"Thanks, kid."

She held up the quetzal feather and twirled it. "You think he can help us with this?"

"We know what it is," Hazel said. She pointed to my phone. "Set up an outing. I want to meet this guy."

I texted everyone, including Shortie. Would this be awkward? I wasn't interested in Harry, but I was a little curious. Shortie might pick up on my feelings. I shook the thoughts from my head and reminded myself I wasn't in middle school.

"So, a quetzal is missing from one of the zoos in Guatemala?" Cynthia studied the feather. She turned it, and it changed colors— green, lime, and even blue.

I took it from her. "It is beautiful."

"Mom?" Cynthia, all wide-eyed innocence, asked. "Think Harry knows about quetzals?"

THE BIRDERS WERE all interested in another outing but couldn't decide where to go. Carmen suggested the Bird Rescue and Care Center, located in a park on Bayou Chico. I never heard of the place, but from her description, it sounded perfect.

I texted Harry where we would meet on Saturday. He worked there when he was in Pensacola and volunteered to be our guide. I didn't know how that would go over with the group, since Owen was our unofficial leader and teacher. Carmen ran a close second in dispensing information.

Saturday, Hazel drove us to the rescue center, Cynthia stuffed in the backseat of her Bug.

"Grandma, this seat is covered in dog fur." Disgust laced her words.

"It's where CB sits," I explained.

"Huh." She wiped the seats with her hands, gathered fur in a clump, and threw it out my window. "Let the birds use it." She brushed off her hands.

Hazel glanced at me. "What do you think Shortie will make of Dr. Morrison?"

I cocked an eyebrow and glared. "Shortie and I are still together, but he has less time for me." *For us.*

"I wonder if Harry has time for you, Mom?" Cynthia tipped her head between the two front seats.

"You look like a turtle sticking its head out." I tapped her on the forehead. "Get back in your seat."

"Anyhow," Hazel chuckled, "this should be a fun day. Beautiful weather. Tell me more about this place."

I opened the Facebook app and went to the Bird Rescue's page. "It says they care for injured or orphaned birds." I scrolled through pictures. "They have a lot of different kinds."

"Not exactly a birding expedition," Cynthia said.

"No, I guess not. Harry said he'd give us a tour, so at least we'll learn more."

Hazel parked, and we climbed out of the Bug.

"This is different," Cynthia said. "I expected more of an office-type place."

I agreed. The building was a faded red brick, one-story residential-style house surrounded by a weathered, white picket fence. Colorful flowers bloomed, attracting butterflies. Mature oak and pine trees provided shade for the picnic benches in the front yard, ready for visitors to relax. Birds called and chirped all around us.

Owen wore his multi-pocket vest and binoculars around his neck, and Carmen was dressed in her typical matchy-matchy outfit. They stood in front of the house.

"We're waiting on Shortie and your young man," he called.

I rolled my eyes. "He is not 'my young man.' I met him at the pool in front of the birding group flyer."

Cynthia pointed to the painted bird footprints on the sidewalk. "How cute."

"This whole place is adorable," Carmen said.

I scanned the parking lot for Harry and Shortie. Behind me, the door to the house slapped closed, and I turned.

"Hi, Peg." Harry raised a hand in greeting. He smiled, showing off a dimple on his right cheek.

How did I miss that? I ignored my finger twitching to trace it. "You got here before us."

Harry introduced himself to the group. His eyes twinkled when he met Hazel, and when he turned, she winked at me.

We made small talk and waited for Shortie. After fifteen minutes, I said, "Let's start. I don't think he's coming. He can catch up if he does."

Hazel hooked her arm through Harry's. "Lead the way, fearless guide." She turned to me and wiggled her eyebrows.

"Your grandmother ..." I gritted my teeth.

Cynthia snickered. "Come on. Don't let me forget to ask him about the feather. I left it in the car."

Harry explained the purpose of the Center and held the door for us to go inside. An older woman sat behind a wooden desk. She wore bright pink lipstick and a matching bow in her teased blonde hair.

"This is Karla Lynch, the face of the Center," Harry said.

She greeted us. "Dr. Harry gives the best tours." She fluttered her eyelashes in his direction. "Y'all have fun."

He smiled, but it didn't reach his eyes. *Her admiration irks him.*

"We're short an employee if it seems messy around here," he continued. "If you know anyone who needs a job, tell them to call me."

"I'm looking for one," Cynthia said. She scribbled her number on a piece of paper and handed it to him.

"Thanks." He pocketed the information. "I'll give you a call."

We explored the exhibits inside, and then Harry led us out the front door and walked before us on a winding outdoor path. He showed us the various cages and areas for different birds. Along the way, signs marked the exhibits and described which bird they held. He led us to the back of the property bordering Bayou Chico, where pelicans and herons played and splashed in the water.

Harry leaned against a fence surrounding a small gazebo-like structure. "This isn't a typical bird-watching outing, but I hope you learned something. Do you have any questions?"

Owen glanced up from his bird checklist. "I have one. Do you work here?"

"No, but I have conducted research with several of these birds, which is why I'm here now. I'm involved in a new area of research."

Owen narrowed his eyes. "I've never seen you at the University."

Harry tipped his head, eyebrows raised. "I've never seen you either."

"*Touché.*" Owen backed down. Dr. Harry's comeback smoothed his ruffled feathers.

Cynthia raised her hand. "I have a question. We found a feather at Fort Pickens. Mr. Owen's book says it's from a quetzal."

Harry's body tensed. "Are you sure?" He turned to Owen, who nodded.

"I can show you," Cynthia said.

Harry swept his hand forward. "After you."

Hazel held out the Bug's keys, and Cynthia retrieved the feather and handed it to Harry.

He twirled it, and the brilliant colors flashed. "Gorgeous," he whispered. He stroked it and peered at Cynthia. "Definitely a quetzal feather, but they don't live in North America. Why was it at the fort, do you think?"

His question, although valid, raised the hair on the back of my neck. The way he looked at the feather was so strange. His manner changed, and his eyes hardened. A shiver ran down my spine. I wasn't sure why

"I don't know much about them. My mom said one went missing from a zoo in Guatemala, and the Kea—"

I took her arm and butted in on their conversation. "It's odd it went missing from a zoo, right?" I couldn't depend on my gut feelings, but I didn't know what else to ask him. He handled the feather in a possessive, creepy way.

"I hadn't read about it." Harry's expression froze.

"It was on the news, Mom said." Cynthia turned to me. "Right? About the Kea—"

Before she said more, I plucked the feather from his grasp, pushed Cynthia to the Bug, opened the door, and forced her into the back seat. "I forgot. We need to go. I have an appointment. See y'all soon." I gestured for Hazel to get in the driver's side, climbed in my seat, and slammed the door.

Hazel turned on the car. "What's the matter, Peg? Why are you acting like this?"

I rubbed my forehead. "I didn't think we should mention the Keatons around Harry. I'm not sure why." I waved my hand. "Come on, let's go."

Hazel sped out of the parking lot. "What about Owen and Carmen? I thought you liked Harry?"

I texted Owen and Carmen. "Yeah, I did. Do. This strange ... sensation ... came over me. Intuition? I'm not sure. He was peculiar. Did you notice his eyes?"

Hazel stopped at a red light. "I didn't, but it's a good idea to pay attention to those gut feelings."

Cynthia piped up from the back seat, "To be honest, he kind of creeped me out."

I turned in my seat. "He did?"

"Yeah. I have a pretty good radar." She studied her fingernails. "But if he's a bird guy, I mean, how bad could he be?"

I chuckled, thinking of Neil and Marla Braden, Sylvia Newman, and Estelle and Roger Keaton. *How bad could a birder be? Ha.*

SHORTIE WAS PARKED in front of my house when we arrived home. He hopped out of his Jeep and made his way down my steep driveway. "Sorry I didn't make it today. I got busy."

"We missed you." He hugged me, and I inhaled his scent— woodsy aftershave—familiar. I relaxed in his arms.

Harry Morrison's dimple flashed through my mind. How could I be interested in him? Was I that shallow? The creep factor from today would not go away. I shook off my thoughts.

Shortie followed us into the house and sat at the island while I got everyone iced tea, and Hazel added water to CB's bowl.

"How'd the tour go?" Shortie sipped his drink and smacked his lips. "You make the best sweet tea."

"Thanks. The tour went well. I guess?"

His eyebrows furrowed. "That doesn't sound good. What happened?"

"The Harry guy was odd," Cynthia said. She leaned against the kitchen counter. "I showed him the quetzal feather. He petted it." She made a face.

Shortie mouthed, "Hairy guy?"

"Very strange," Hazel agreed.

"Mom wouldn't let me talk about the Keatons." Cynthia chewed on her thumbnail. "Why, Mom?"

"Harry, Shortie." I spelled Dr. Morrison's first name, and his confused expression cleared. To Cynthia, I said, "Like I said in the car, I got some kind of strange feeling. I don't know how else to explain it." A dark heaviness filled me when he held the feather. His reaction didn't sit right.

Shortie shook his head. "Trust your gut."

"Same thing I said." Hazel refilled her tea and offered everyone more.

Sure, because my gut always took me to safe places. "What kept you busy today?" I changed the subject.

He tapped the countertop with his hands. "Looking for my first car to flip."

"Cool. What did you find?" Cynthia said.

They chatted about cars while I considered Harry's reaction to the feather. Why would a quetzal feather be at an old fort? And near where Hazel discovered Roger Keaton's body? It didn't make sense to me. The bird disappeared from the zoo in Guatemala months ago, and the Keatons were spotted in Pensacola a few days ago.

If those two things were linked, where was the quetzal kept all this time? Who smuggled the bird into the United States, the Keatons? Or someone else?

"How would they get the bird into the country?" I said aloud.

Shortie and Cynthia looked up from their discussion.

"Huh?" My daughter's quizzical expression reminded me of her dad.

"The Keatons. If they stole the bird last fall, where has it been? Where have they been? How did they carry it into the U.S.? Is it possible someone else brought it here?"

Hazel hurried to her room and returned with a notebook and pen. She pulled out a chair at the table. "Let's sit over here, Peg. They can talk cars. I'm with you on this investigation. None of it makes sense."

I sat, and CB curled up at my feet. I tapped her notebook. "No, it doesn't. Plus, if Roger and Estelle snatched the bird from the zoo, why? What point would it be to steal it, keep it for a while, and then bring it here?"

She raised her finger. "Most important of all, who killed Roger Keaton?"

Chapter 7

Hazel clicked her pen, flipped to a clean page, and wrote *QUETZAL MYSTERY* in all caps at the top. "We should put our questions in chronological order of how things happened."

"Okay," I said. "First, the bird went missing back in the fall. It was on the television right after it happened."

She scribbled the information and glanced up. "What zoo did it come from?"

I hunted for the answer on my cell phone. "I'm not positive it came from a zoo. Wait, from what I'm reading, it says yes, someone stole the bird from one of the Guatemalan zoos. Doesn't say which one. Maybe they wanted to keep it a secret?"

She made more notes. "What happened next?"

"The day of Chloe's baby shower, we found out the Keatons were back in Pensacola." I checked my calendar app. "Cynthia picked up the feather last Saturday, and you found Roger's body."

Hazel winced. "Not fun."

"I know." And I did, from personal experience. "Today, a week later, Dr. Harry got all weird about the feather."

She finished writing and set down her pen. "Where do we start?"

"The quetzal is at the heart of this. Roger was a notorious bad guy. He had a reputation, but after all these years, why was he murdered now? Let's check the local channel and see if they have any updates on his death."

I turned on the television. Shortie and Cynthia joined us, and Hazel explained what we were searching for. I ordered two pizzas—our traditional pepperoni and deluxe—and texted Chloe to ask how she felt.

"Nothing new," she responded. "Baby hasn't dropped, but I have a doctor's appointment on Monday. Can you take me? Tom has a meeting."

I confirmed when to pick her up. The news began, but there were no reports about the quetzal or the Keatons. When the pizza arrived, I passed out paper plates and napkins and set the boxes on the coffee table so we could watch television while we ate.

"We should find out more about quetzals," Cynthia said. She bit into her slice and spoke around her food. "Why was one taken? They're not pets, right?"

Shortie wiped his mouth with his napkin. "I'll say it again. I don't think we need to be involved in this."

I took a huge bite, chewed, and swallowed. "You have to admit you're curious, or you wouldn't still be here."

He grunted, a sheepish expression on his face.

I wiggled my eyebrows. I knew him better than he thought.

"Mom, what kind of research is Harry involved in?" Cynthia stood and gathered our trash. "He never said. Could it have to do with quetzals?"

"Quite a stretch, don't you think?" Shortie said.

"Not really," I said. "He is at a bird sanctuary."

"I can call and ask." Hazel whipped out her cell phone. "What's his number, Peg?"

Shortie raised an eyebrow. "You have his number?"

"I have Owen's too." I patted his hand. "Trust me, this guy is strange."

"That's not comforting either." Shortie yawned. "I'm going home. Text me if y'all find out more. Carter still moving back tomorrow?"

I nodded. Two of my kids would be living under my roof. The thought warmed me. "I'll walk you out."

He kissed me goodbye on the porch and trotted up my steep front yard to his Jeep. How had I ever considered Harry over Shortie? Ugh, men. I shook my head and went back inside, locking the door behind me.

Cynthia sat at the table jotting notes in Hazel's notebook. "Whatcha doing?"

She leaned back so I could read what she had written. "While you walked Shortie out, I went online to look up quetzals. How much do you know about them?"

"We learned a little when we first heard one went missing," I said.

Hazel joined us at the table. "I'll call Dr. Harry on Monday. Cynthia, what have you found?"

My daughter raised her finger and read from her notes. "Quetzals live mostly in tropical forests in Guatemala, Mexico, and Central America. One other thing I learned is they hop between the trees."

"I remember that from last year's news report," I said.

"It also says they don't do well in captivity. So, if the Keatons did steal one, they didn't care."

That also fit with what I knew about the couple.

"What else have you discovered?" Hazel asked.

Cynthia tapped on her phone. "There are five species. What

this article describes sounds like I found a resplendent quetzal feather. The bird's tail is long and blue-green in color."

"Is the species endangered?" I pulled out a chair and sat.

"Near threatened, it says. Because of deforestation." She narrowed her eyebrows. "Would the Keatons have known this?"

"What does near threatened mean? And I have no idea. They were not good people. If they knew, why did they take the bird?" I never heard that they cared about the environment. Maybe they wanted to breed quetzals?

Cynthia looked up my first question. "Okay, it means the quetzals might become endangered in the near future."

I nodded. "That makes sense."

Hazel piped up, "What if they planned to breed them?"

"That was my thought. Could they do that?" I asked.

Cynthia used her phone again to find the information we wanted. "It looks like an aquarium in Texas received eggs from a place in Mexico about twenty years ago. The eggs hatched and were the first resplendent quetzals to hatch in captivity."

"That would take a lot of equipment, and I don't picture the Keatons doing it. Plus, you'd need a pair of quetzals to mate them." I leaned back in my chair and rubbed the back of my neck.

"Wasn't the Spanish galleon from Mexico?" Hazel said.

"Caravel," I corrected. "They're smaller than a galleon. How could that be related?" We were searching too hard for a link between the Keatons and the quetzal. I doubted the discovery of a five-hundred-year-old ship had anything to do with them.

She raised her hands and shrugged. "Making connections."

"Okay, weird idea. Cloning?"

"Cloning? Wouldn't that take even more work?" Hazel's eyebrows reached her bangs.

"Yeah, it would," I said with a sigh.

"Definitely," Cynthia agreed.

Why were the Keatons in the States? What did a quetzal have to do with them? Considering their pasts, I knew it might, but I couldn't connect them.

Hazel stood. "I'm tired. This isn't getting us anywhere."

"Me too." I yawned and stretched. "Cynth, are you staying up?"

"I'll keep researching these birds. And the ship."

I nodded and reached for my cell phone. It rang, and the screen read, "Unknown." My blood froze.

"Mom? What's wrong? Why are you so pale?" Cynthia jumped up and motioned for me to sit.

"Hazel, it says "Unknown." My hand trembled when I set the phone on the table.

"Answer it," my daughter said. "When Dr. Harry called, it said that."

Hazel rushed over. "Wait, what if ... what if it's her?" Her voice dropped to a whisper.

"Who?" Cynthia clicked accept and speaker. "Hello?"

"It's me again."

It wasn't Harry Morrison this time. My anonymous caller was back. Was it Estelle Keaton, like Neil Braden said last fall? Or someone else?

I stabbed the red circle to hang up. "Nope, not talking to whoever that is." I powered down my phone, set it on the table, and backed away, hands in the air. "I'm going to have to call Marcus."

CARTER ARRIVED Sunday mid-morning with his car packed full. It took several trips to put all his belongings into his room.

Cynthia teased him about having so much, but I reminded her that she had brought home even more. When we were finished, Carter waved us out of his room, explaining he needed a nap.

"You're not going to put your things away?"

"Mom, I have lived in a dorm for the past year. I've got this." He shut the door.

Okay, then.

"Will you call Marcus now?" Hazel stood beside me, wringing her hands. "This is too much like last year. We've already found one dead body."

"That was *you*," I pointed out. I wasn't taking responsibility for all the bodies.

"Right. But last time, *you* found them, and it was two dead people. Remember?"

I hadn't forgotten. I sighed and held out my hand. "Can I use your phone? Mine is still turned off." I didn't want to turn it back on. My skin crawled, remembering the call from the night before.

I told Cynthia about the anonymous caller. She was unhappy that I kept the information from her and waited while I spoke to Marcus.

He answered with a gruff "Hello" and said he'd come right over. I made a pot of coffee and slouched on the couch. This wasn't how I wanted to end my weekend. I stood, opened the vertical blinds over the back sliding door, and went outside. I clutched the deck's railing, inhaled and exhaled hard, and prayed my beautiful backyard and the birds and critters would bring me peace.

"You okay?" Lauree called from her porch.

I turned at her voice. "Yeah."

My single-word answer didn't convince either of us. My friend tiptoed around the kids' toys in her yard and climbed the steps to my deck. She raised an eyebrow. "What happened?"

"How much time do you have?" Car tires sounded on my driveway, and I held up a hand. "Marcus is here. Why don't you sit in on our conversation? It'll be interesting."

Lauree didn't say a word. She followed me into the house and closed the sliding door behind her. Hazel let Marcus in. CB joined us at the table, wagging his behind whenever the detective looked in his direction.

"Fill me in, Peg." Marcus smirked, skepticism filling his voice.

"After Hazel found Roger Keaton's body, Shortie and I went to the beach to eat and saw a black sedan. Like Estelle Keaton's."

Marcus raised an eyebrow.

"It had an orange license plate. We looked for the car, but we didn't find it. Then, I met Dr. Harry, who gave us a tour of the Bird Rescue and Care Center. He was weird."

Marcus blinked twice. "Dr. Hairy?"

I spelled it for him like I had for Shortie. "He has a Ph.D. in wildlife with a specialty in ornithology. He studies birds. Anyhow, we—" I gestured from Cynthia to Hazel to myself. "Started talking about Roger and the quetzal. It's possible the Keatons brought the bird into the U.S. to breed or clone it."

"Clone?" His lips twitched. "Where does this Harry guy come into this?"

"Yes, cloning. I'm telling you what happened. There was the ship they discovered, and it might contain gold or treasure."

I couldn't read his expression.

"The thing is … why I called you … well, someone called me last night." I picked at the skin around my thumb.

"And?"

I blew out a heavy sigh. "My anonymous caller, Marcus. He's back."

Marcus was less than thrilled by my news. Lauree either. He left with a promise to check my phone records and try to find out who had called me. Lauree hugged me tight and stepped back.

"I am not sure what to say." She shook her head. "Please be careful. This is too much like last time. And you have a grandbaby coming."

I hadn't forgotten. It wasn't like I wanted these things to happen. "I'll be careful."

Her face said she wasn't sure she believed me. She left, and I pushed the chairs back in place. "Anyone want some lunch?"

MONDAY MORNING, I picked up Chloe for her appointment. I scooted her seat back to give her more leg and belly room. She looked as if the baby had dropped. I was curious what the doctor would say. I let her out at the hospital's entrance, parked, and joined her inside the lobby. I pushed thoughts of the anonymous caller from my mind. Lauree was right. I had a grandbaby on the way, and that's where I needed to focus.

I looped my arm through Chloe's as we walked to the doctor's office. "Want to go shopping after?"

She stopped and glared at me. "I feel like this kiddo will drop out right here. My back hurts, my feet hurt. So, no. No shopping."

I bit back a grin, remembering that miserable feeling. She checked in with the receptionist, and we sat on hard wooden chairs, with half a dozen other pregnant women, and waited. And waited. After over an hour, a nurse came out and apologized to us all, explaining the doctor had an emergency but would see patients soon.

Chloe grunted and looked down. "I think I qualify as an emergency too."

I followed her gaze and realized her water had broken. "Oh, my. Oh. Well, let's get you to the hospital."

"We *are* at the hospital," she said through gritted teeth.

The nurse found a wheelchair and maneuvered us through the halls from the doctor's office area to labor and delivery. I texted Tom and Hazel to come ASAP. I hadn't given birth in over eighteen years, and now my baby was having a baby. Life was changing fast.

Chapter 8

Tom ran so fast into the birthing room that he slid to a stop inside the door. Sweat dripped off his forehead. "Are you okay?" he asked Chloe before turning to me. "Is she okay?"

I held out my hands. "Calm down. She's doing well."

Chloe chose that moment to groan.

His eyes grew wide, and he knelt beside her bed. "What can I do? I brought the bag." He looked around the room. "It's in the car?" He stood. "I'll go find it."

Mexican jumping beans had nothing on Tom.

I put my hand on his shoulder. "Give me your keys, and I'll go. Calm down. We'll be here awhile."

A male nurse walked in, and I pulled him to the side. "Can you reassure the dad? He's kind of freaking out."

"I got him," he said.

My emotions bounced everywhere as I walked toward the elevator. A baby. My grandson or granddaughter would be here soon. I didn't even try to suppress my excitement. I wrapped my arms around myself and held the joy and anticipation close. The elevator doors opened on the ground floor, and I spotted Cynthia, Carter, and Hazel entering the building.

"I'm getting Chloe's bag from Tom's car." I held his keys in the air.

"We're going to the gift shop for balloons." Cynthia linked arms with Hazel. "And whatever else Grandma finds." She giggled.

"A stuffed bear or bunny too," Hazel said.

Carter winced. "I'll come with you, Mom."

His trapped expression tickled me. Who knew how long we had to wait before the baby came? Carter wouldn't be interested in hanging around through the process. He followed me to the parking lot.

"Can you run to the house for my digital camera? It takes the best pictures." A job would give him an escape. I pointed to where my car sat, two rows over next to a white van, and held out my keys.

"Yes." He blew out a breath. "Thank you." He kissed my cheek and trotted off. "Tell Chloe I'll come back soon," he called over his shoulder.

"No problem. Take your time."

I wasn't too excited about seeing my daughter in pain either. I had clear memories of giving birth to all three kids, Zack by my side.

"You would be the best Pop," I whispered. I bit my lips to stop the trembling—no more crying. If Zack were here, he would do cartwheels. I couldn't do those, but I could jump for joy.

My phone rang as my feet hit the ground, and Shortie's name showed. I swiped my cheeks, sniffled, and cleared my throat. "Hey, guess what?"

"Baby's coming?"

"How'd you know?" I asked.

"Just a guess. Is it happening now?"

"I'm getting her bag from Tom's car. He's a mess." I unlocked the vehicle, leaned in, and found Chloe's suitcase.

"I remember when Kim was born. I passed out, and they used smelling salts." He had a smile in his voice.

"I can't imagine." His story distracted me from missing Zack.

"Yes. Her mom stayed calm, cool, and collected, like always. Not me, though."

"You were a big baby, huh?"

"Pretty much. I'll come by after work, but I'm out of there if she's in pain or screaming."

"Got it." I locked the car. "I'll text Lauree. She can check on CB and Roscoe if we're here long."

We said our goodbyes, and I hung up, still chuckling at Shortie's story. Who would imagine he'd pass out when his baby was born? His daughter, Kim, lifeguarded at UWF. She and my girls attended the same high school. I had never met Shortie's ex-wife, though he told me a little about her. My imagination went wild, concocting a whole story about meeting her, and then I went on to compare Shortie and Dr. Harry.

Lost in my thoughts, I jumped when my phone dinged. I opened it to find a message from Hazel.

BABY IS COMING. NOW.

Sweat broke out all over my body, and my heart rate spiked. "The baby is coming." The news penetrated my brain, and I broke into a jog. I entered the hospital and pounded the *Up* button for the elevator.

"Hurry up." I danced in place. "Come on, come on. We have a baby on the way."

The doors opened. I jumped inside and hit the floor

number for Labor and Delivery and the *Close Door* button one after the other. My hands shook as I texted Shortie, Lauree, and Carter. The elevator arrived on the birthing center floor, and I took off, skidded around a corner, and stuttered to a stop inside Chloe's room.

And witnessed the most amazing, precious, heart-stopping moment—my baby giving birth.

Tom and the nurse stood on each side of Chloe, coaching her to push. The doctor waited to deliver my grandchild. I joined Hazel and Cynthia, and we locked hands.

"Wow." I didn't have any other words at the moment.

The doctor maneuvered the baby's head and shoulders. He caught him, announced, "It's a boy," and placed him on Chloe's chest. Hazel, Cynthia, and I wrapped our arms around each other and let Tom and Chloe enjoy their new family.

After several minutes, Chloe called me over. "Mom, come meet Reese."

I swallowed the lump in my throat, tiptoed to the bedside, and touched the blanket wrapped around him. "Reese. I love the name."

"Reese Zackary," Tom said with a watery smile.

Hazel joined me. "He's beautiful. Your dad would be so proud."

Cynthia circled the bed and hugged Chloe. The two cried together, and we all celebrated this new little life. Tom handed the baby to me, and after I kissed his head, I passed him to his great-grandmother. He made the rounds, and I took him back again. I sat and unwrapped his blanket, counted his fingers and toes, and stroked his wispy reddish-brown hair. He stared at me with wise eyes. I leaned close so he could focus on my face.

"Reese, my sweet boy. I'm your grandma. I'm going to spoil you and love you, no matter what. I'll always be here for you."

He wrapped his fingers around my pinky. I smiled through my tears, and I sensed a release. The love I felt right then expanded and covered the fear that had haunted me since Zack's death. I saw the future in this tiny baby's eyes, one of love and freedom —no more fear of what might happen. Possibilities and relationships were unlocked. My heart opened. "Every day, sweet boy. Every day, I will pray for you. I love you." I kissed his forehead, and he closed his eyes.

The peace that passes understanding, the one Paul talked about in Philippians, covered our family.

EARLY THE NEXT MORNING, I sat on the couch, still in my PJs, a mug of coffee in one hand and thoughts of baby Reese warming my heart. My phone rang, and *Unknown* popped up.

I had been riding the high of Reese's birth through the night and into the new day, and this person had plopped their dark and dreary self into my life. I was tired of being afraid.

"Hello," I shouted into the phone. "I don't know who you are, but you better quit calling me. I've told the police all about you." I hit the end call button and sat back, feeling validated. I am woman. Hear me roar.

Hazel peeked around the corner from her room, eyebrows drawn together, hair sticking up in all directions. "You okay?"

"I am great." I slapped my legs and stood. "Want some coffee?"

"Sure." She drew the word out.

Ignoring her questioning look, I went into the kitchen, pulled out four mugs, filled the coffeepot with water, and set it up to brew. While waiting, I straightened up the kitchen, unloaded the dishwasher, and took out a package of ground beef for dinner.

I didn't care what anyone said or did. Grandma was my new title, and no one would mess with me. Hazel and Cynthia would help me find out who killed Roger and find the missing quetzal.

And then, I was finished solving mysteries.

My phone rang again. This time, Chloe's name showed. I set it on the island and hit the speaker button.

"Hi, honey. How are you? How's the baby?" I poured coffee into two cups, handed Hazel hers, and sipped from mine. "Yesterday was amazing, wasn't it? Tom texted me earlier and told me you wanted the morning to yourself to rest. Anything you need?"

"I'm okay ... but Mom?" Her voice wobbled.

"What's wrong?" My stomach dropped, and the coffee burned a trail down my throat. I set down my mug. "Is Reese all right? I thought he was in the nursery so that you could nap."

She moaned. "Yes, the baby is fine. He is in the nursery right now. But ... but, I have a visitor."

Hazel frowned. "What's wrong?" she mouthed.

I shrugged. "Who is it, Chloe? You're scaring me." Who would make her react this way?

A voice came over the line. One I knew well. "Hi, Peg."

Hazel was mid-sip and spilled her coffee when she heard the voice.

My heart raced, and the tiny hairs on the back of my neck stood up. I put my hand over my phone. "Call Marcus," I hissed.

She rushed off to her room.

I took a deep breath and said, "You leave that room right now. The police know who you are." I gritted my teeth. They better not hurt my daughter or my grandson.

Scuffling noises sounded through the speaker, and a door slammed shut.

"Chloe? Chloe, are you there?" I squeezed the phone.

"I'm here, Mom." Chloe's voice grew stronger. "That person. Someone. I couldn't tell who it was."

"Chloe," I interrupted, "hit your nurse's button. Now!" I didn't want the intruder to escape. I gripped my phone tighter. "They need to lock down the hospital."

The nursing station answered her page, and Chloe explained what happened. An alarm rang out with the words "Code Silver."

"I did it." Tears filled her voice. "Who was it? Why did they make me call you?"

Nausea rolled through my gut. Did my yelling into my phone earlier cause this? *Oh, Lord,* I prayed. *Keep my babies safe.*

Hazel hurried to me. "Sit, Peg. Come on, now." She eased the phone from my hand and guided me to the couch, then pushed my head between my knees. "Breathe. Chloe is safe. Marcus is on the way, and I called Shortie."

Breathe, breathe. They're safe. I repeated the words over and over while Hazel talked to Chloe.

How did this happen? Who was this person? I tugged Hazel's shirt. "Ask what they looked like."

She kept her hand on my back. "Can you describe the person to me?" Her voice remained calm and controlled.

I focused on my breathing and listened to Chloe's answer.

"No, Grandma. They were dressed in black and had one of those balaclava things that cover everything but the eyes and mouth."

Hazel released me, and I sat up, eyes closed, taking measured breaths. Someone put a glass in my hand, and I opened my eyes.

"Drink." Cynthia gestured to the water I held. She put her arm around me. "You're okay. Chloe is safe."

Tears trickled down her cheeks. I lifted a shaky hand and wiped them away. "Thank you."

She sniffled. "Grandma Hazel is waking Carter, and we're all going to the hospital. Do you think you can get your things together? Do you need help?"

I inhaled and exhaled hard. She helped me stand and made me wait for the room to stop spinning. I managed to put on some clothes and brush my teeth. Afterward, I stood lost in thought. Images raced through my mind. What should I do next?

Hazel opened my bedroom door. "You're dressed, good. Put on your shoes." She pointed, and I slipped my feet into an old pair of sneakers. She held out my bag. "Here's your purse. Come on, now. The kids are waiting."

I followed her into the garage and sat beside her in the back seat of my SUV. Cynthia drove, and Carter sat in the front passenger seat. He turned around and patted my knee. "Mom?"

His worried expression broke me. My strength evaporated, and I slumped in my seat.

This stranger, the *Unknown Caller*, had kicked my legs out from under me.

Chapter 9

When we arrived at the hospital, I hurried into the downstairs bathroom and peered in the mirror. Bags under the eyes, check. Tear stains on the cheeks, check. Defeated posture, check. This all needed to change.

Chloe's safety was the priority right now. I splashed my face with cold water and dried it on stiff brown paper towels. Lotion and lip balm would help, but they were hiding somewhere at the bottom of my purse. I rummaged around until I found them. Both helped my skin appear brighter. I forced a strained smile at my reflection.

"That'll have to do." I straightened up, stretched my neck side to side, inhaled, and exhaled hard. "I can do this." I squared my shoulders and left the bathroom.

The kids and Hazel waited for me. Hazel waved me into an elevator and pushed the *Up* arrow. I spotted Shortie running into the building and stuck out my hand to stop the door.

"Here we are," I hollered.

We hugged, and he held my hand, but I refused to let my emotions dominate the situation.

"Marcus should be here by now," I said.

Shortie nodded and squeezed my hand tighter. "No idea why the person was here?"

"No, not for sure," I hedged.

The elevator shimmied to a halt on Chloe's floor, and we got off. We walked five steps, and a nurse approached us.

"Can I see your IDs, please?" Her no-nonsense expression and stance calmed some of my fears.

I explained who we were, and we showed our identification. She led us around the corner, motioning to another nurse who walked us to a different room than Chloe had been in the day before. An armed guard sat in a plastic chair beside the door.

The nurse said softly, "Your daughter is safe. We've moved her to this interior room. The baby is with her, and a guard will be stationed outside her room until they are released from the hospital."

Shortie held the door, and I spotted Chloe propped up in her bed, Reese snug in her arms. Tom sat against the bed, between the door and his wife and child.

My lips trembled, and I bit my tongue. No tears, not now. I opened my arms and hugged my daughter and grandson. I patted Tom's shoulder. "Y'all okay, now?" My words came out scratchy.

"What is this about, Mom?" Chloe's hands shook as she smoothed the blanket around the baby.

I didn't know how to answer her. When I yelled, it must have triggered the anonymous caller to take this drastic step.

The door opened, and Marcus Sharp stepped inside.

"I'm so sorry, honey. This is all my fault." I backed away from the bed.

Everyone in the room froze.

Shortie touched my arm. "No, it's not, Peg. You didn't do this."

"I yelled at the person, though. They called earlier today." They needed to understand what triggered this.

"Doesn't matter. You didn't cause this." Shortie wrapped his arms around me.

"He's right. Remember last time? This person is unhinged," Marcus said.

What they said might be true, but it didn't help. At all.

"We've searched everywhere but didn't find anyone here who doesn't belong." Marcus turned to Chloe and flipped his notebook open. "Tell me in detail what happened and what the person said."

I listened to her account. She couldn't tell if the person was male or female, but she guessed height and weight.

Before she finished talking, someone knocked on the door. Shortie opened it, and the guard stuck his head in.

"Sir," he addressed Marcus, "they found a black balaclava in the trash can by the back parking lot."

Marcus nodded, lips pursed, eyes narrowed. The guard closed the door, and Marcus's gaze swung to me, his eyes flashing with questions. "This person called you again?"

"This morning. I told them off." I hung my head, and guilt filled my body.

He shrugged. "Don't blame you there."

Hazel's mouth dropped open. "He's human," she whispered.

I elbowed her. Now was not the time. "Thanks," I said to Marcus. "I think it set them off."

He flipped his notebook shut and slipped it into his back pocket. "We may never know. Anyhow, we'll have a guard stationed here until tomorrow. The doctor indicated your daughter can go home then."

Shortie stepped forward. "Do you think they need someone at their house?"

"They shouldn't. Peg ... er, Mrs. Howard, seems to be the intended ..." The detective's neck reddened.

Target. I knew what he wanted to say.

He turned to leave, but Hazel patted his arm.

"Wait a minute." She touched my hand. "Come with us." She pushed Marcus out into the hall, and I traipsed after them.

We stepped around the corner, and Hazel held up her hands. "We think Harry Morrison is somehow involved with this."

I almost blurted out, "We do?" but held my tongue.

Marcus's eyebrows drew together. "You told me about him two days ago. I don't see how he would be involved. You're making assumptions."

"He's weird," I said. I wasn't as convinced as Hazel about Harry's involvement. If so, my zing and zap feelings and the dimple were all a ruse, and I couldn't trust my feelings. I tuned back into their conversation.

Marcus's lips tipped into a grin. "Can't arrest someone for weirdness."

Hazel stomped her foot. "No, he's very unusual. Peculiar even. You need to check into him. We showed him the quetzal feather, and ... and he was creepy."

His mouth twisted to the side. "You told me. Again, I can't arrest someone for creepiness."

"Ugh." Hazel huffed and turned to me. "He doesn't understand."

I linked my arm through hers and tugged her back toward Chloe's room. "It's okay, Marcus. Don't worry about it."

"What are you doing?" Hazel jerked her arm from mine. "We need him to realize what Harry is like."

I stopped. "Do you really think Harry is the caller?"

She stepped back. "Well ... no."

"This person, this caller, thinks they've won and scared us

into coming here. They think they can threaten my child and grandchild." I stood tall, shoulders back, head high. "No one bullies my people."

WE DIDN'T STAY LONG at the hospital. Chloe and Tom were exhausted, and little Reese kept fussing, probably in reaction to all the tension in the room.

I couldn't believe the caller had the gall to sneak into the hospital. "They'll check all the cameras?" I asked Shortie. We exited and headed for our cars.

He pulled me close and kissed my temple. "Yes, they will. Marcus isn't stupid."

I raised an eyebrow. He wasn't dumb and had the backing of the entire Pensacola Police Department. But this was my family. My grandbaby.

Shortie had some work to finish and said he'd come over afterward. All I wanted was to go back to bed and pretend this hadn't happened. Cynthia and Carter overruled me and stopped for takeout at a local restaurant that served pub grub.

"I'm staying in the car, but I want a Philly cheesesteak," I said.

Carter tapped my order into his phone. "Grandma?"

She tilted her head back and closed her eyes. "Tell him, Peg."

"She wants the half muffuletta."

"Got it." Cynthia opened the windows and handed me the keys. "We'll be right back."

I closed my eyes and tipped my head against the headrest. "What a day."

Hazel snored.

The car door opened. I screamed and then realized it was my kids.

Carter held up a bag and shook it. "It's us, Mom."

I swiped a bit of drool from my chin. Beside me, Hazel straightened and yawned.

"I think I fell asleep."

"You snore." I teased her.

Our heavy moods lightened. We headed to the house. After we ate lunch, Cynthia cleaned up, and I stretched out on the couch. Her phone rang, and when she finished her conversation, she came and sat on the coffee table beside me.

"Mom? Remember I gave Harry my number because he needed extra help? He called me."

I opened an eye. "Dr. Harry?"

She nodded.

"What did he want?"

"He offered me a job." She studied her fingernails. "I think I'll take it."

I sat up and ran my fingers through my hair. "What does he want you to do?"

"He said he needed someone to take notes on his current project. Some kind of bird research, I guess." She stood. "He asked if I would be able to start Monday."

"You said yes?" She said she thought she'd take it, but I knew my daughter.

"I did. I know you think he's weird."

"You said you did too. He creeped us out."

"Yes, I did. I do. Grandma wanted to ask him about quetzals. So, I thought I could investigate while I'm working."

I closed my eyes. This girl. Some would say she took after her mother.

∿

MONDAY MORNING, I dropped Cynthia off at the Bird Rescue and scanned the parking lot for Harry. "Text me when you are ready to leave. I'm headed for Chloe's."

"Oh, give Reese kisses from me." She slung her backpack over her shoulder.

She walked up to the office, and I leaned out my window. "Cynthia?"

She turned, eyebrows raised in question.

"Be careful."

She winked and walked off. It reminded me of kindergarten drop-off—the first day. She thought she was a grownup. Technically, now she was. But what she didn't understand was that she'd always be my baby, and I had to protect my babies.

I left to visit my middle kiddo and my grandson. Joy soared inside me. The *Unknown Caller* would not steal that from me. I drove over the bridge from Pensacola to Gulf Breeze while my mind churned out suspects. I narrowed it down to Estelle Keaton, but she hadn't acted alone last time. She used Neil Braden, Pensacola's mayor at the time, as her pawn. She may have been the mastermind behind it all, but she didn't get her hands dirty. That was all Neil.

Assuming she still held her leadership position in the bad guy group, who did she control this time? Why were the police unable to find her? I couldn't see any relationship between Dr. Harry and her. No link at all. Being odd didn't make him a killer. That was silly thinking on my part. There wasn't anyone else. Of course, last time, I hadn't been aware of Neil right away. I hoped they would catch Estelle—and soon.

I tapped my steering wheel before pulling into Chloe's driveway and parking the car. A low-level sense of dread sat in my stomach, but I couldn't pin down why.

"I'm not taking this inside," I said aloud with a shake of my shoulders. "No darkness around the sweet baby."

Chloe and Reese were napping, so I volunteered to help Tom. He started a load of laundry while I cleaned up the kitchen and emptied the overflowing trashcan. He entered the room as I cleaned the counters.

"Babies make a lot of laundry." He pulled out a chair and plopped into it.

"Tired?"

He used his fingers to pry his eyes open. "Can you tell?"

I chuckled. "Go lay down. If Reese wakes up, I can change him and hold him."

He pushed himself up. "Thank you, Peg. Sure wish my mom was still alive. She'd have loved Reese." He headed for the master bedroom.

While they napped, I dusted and straightened up. Afterward, I curled up on the couch. My phone pinged with a text from Cynthia.

> So far, so good. Dr. Harry is okay today.
> He has a helper, Kurt. He's kinda cute.
> His stepsister, Gabby, works here too.
> She's weird.

She added a wink emoji.

> My eyes are open for bad guy stuff.

I shook my head and answered her with a smiley face. Cynthia didn't date much in high school, and then she went straight into the Navy. She never shared her love life with me, and I didn't ask. Maybe this Kurt fellow would be a part of it.

Reese cried, and all thoughts of boyfriends left. I tiptoed into Chloe and Tom's bedroom and picked him up. Chloe stirred and opened one eye.

"Mom?"

"I got him. You rest." I pulled the door shut behind me.

I found the diaper bag and changed the baby, then I wrapped him up and tucked him in the crook of my arm. "Hi, sweet boy," I crooned. We sat for a while, studying each other. I baby-talked to him and counted his toes and fingers. I was in the middle of singing "Itsy Bitsy Spider" when Chloe entered the room.

"Having fun?"

"The best." I picked Reese up and snuggled him before handing him to his mamma. "Sleep well?"

She settled in to nurse her son. He latched on, and she leaned back. "I dreamed someone chased me. And Reese went missing." She brushed her hair away from the baby's fingers. "That person at the hospital scared me."

"I'm so sorry, honey."

She made a face. "You want to be in the birding group and all. I understand, I do. But this stuff with killers and anonymous calls ..." She readjusted the baby. "You need to be more careful."

I agreed with her. People kept saying it, but I already knew. Chasing killers wasn't what I wanted to do. But I couldn't figure out how to stop.

Chapter 10

Chloe fed the baby and handed him to me to hold while she dressed. She entered the room, twirling her hair into a messy bun. "Want to take a walk?"

"Yes, let's get out of here." A change of perspective sounded great. Maybe I could shake off the feeling that another shoe was about to drop.

We stepped outside, and my hair frizzed and stuck to my face. "Oh, this humidity. Summer is on the way."

"Memorial Day was last week," Chloe said.

I hadn't even thought of that. We'd been so busy with the baby and the caller. "Hmm. We didn't do anything."

"Yeah."

We rounded the corner and strolled up the road.

"Hurricane season starts soon," I said.

Chloe stopped and giggled, holding her belly. "We are discussing the weather, Mom. I just had a baby, and here we are, like two old women, talking about the temperature and holidays."

I joined her in giggling. "Sorry. My mind is in a fog."

She sobered up and started walking. "I know what you mean."

"You can blame yours on baby hormones, though." I sighed. My foggy thoughts came from worrying about Estelle Keaton and her next step.

"True. So, tell me what's going on."

Where to start? "Did I tell you about Dr. Harry?"

"No. Who's he?" Reese fussed, and she adjusted his blanket. "Let's head back. I think he needs his diaper changed."

"Sure." We turned around. "So, Dr. Harry. He's a bird specialist. Your sister started working for him today."

She stopped and stared at me. "You sound funny. Tell me more about this guy."

"He's ... handsome. He has a dimple."

She cocked an eyebrow. "We like dimples?"

I ignored her comment. "He's smart too. Knows all about birds. But he's kind of weird."

"Good-looking but weird. Not a rave review. What about Shortie?"

I had thought about this more and wondered if I had gotten too comfortable with Shortie. Had I settled? Nice, handsome guy who liked me, and I "fell" into the relationship. I hadn't made a decision to date after ten years. It happened.

Maybe I was short-changing us, though. He was a great guy, and I thought I loved him. I opened my mouth to respond as we turned the corner onto her street, but what I saw stopped me.

"Do you know anyone with a black car?" I gestured to the vehicle parked at the curb in front of her house.

"Not like that one."

A person dressed in all black got out of the sedan, tucked something in the mailbox, jumped back into the car, and gunned the engine, speeding away. Alarm bells rang in my brain. Did it have an orange license plate? I gripped Chloe's arm and pulled her to a stop.

"You and Reese stay here." We were three houses from hers. I took my phone from my back pocket and called Marcus's number.

"Peg?"

"Someone put a package in Chloe's mailbox," I said.

"Okay …"

"Black car, orange plate, I think."

His sigh echoed through the line. "Peg …" he began.

I marched to the mailbox and jerked it open. Inside sat a gift box wrapped in blue paper. I pulled it out and discovered an envelope with Reese's name. I explained what I found to Marcus, hit the speaker button, and put my phone inside the mailbox, leaving the door open so he could hear me.

I ripped open the envelope. "I'm checking the card."

He grunted.

I tugged the card out. My hands shook as I opened it and read the words out loud. "Reese, welcome to the world. I saw you all snug as a bug in the nursery. Tell your grandma I'll call soon." Bile rose in my throat, and I gagged. My anonymous caller brought this.

"Marcus." I clutched my phone, but words escaped me. Icy fingers scraped down my back. I plopped onto the driveway.

"On the way, Peg. What's the address?"

I whispered the information and hung up. Chloe approached. She held Reese against her chest and patted his back.

"Mom?"

I closed my eyes. "The person in the car?" I looked up at her and shaded my eyes with my hand. "I think it was the person who got into your hospital room."

Chloe clutched Reese closer and backed up. "What?"

I pushed myself off the ground and hugged her and the baby. "The police are on the way, honey." No new mom needed this kind of stress. I left the stroller by the front door and followed her into the house.

Reese's diaper sagged on his little behind. I took him from Chloe and cleaned him up, adding a fresh diaper and swaddling him. Tom stumbled out of the bedroom, hair sticking up in all directions. I wanted to say something funny, like "Hello, Einstein," but I couldn't bring myself to do it. Humor didn't seem appropriate right now.

He stopped and frowned. "What's wrong?"

Chloe slumped onto the couch. "That person." She waved her hand. "The one from the hospital. He stopped by the house ..." She choked on her words and broke into sobs.

Tom rushed to her side and held her in his arms. "What is going on?"

I cuddled Reese to my chest, swaying to quiet his worried cries. "She's right." I told him about our walk, seeing the car, and the person who put a package in the mailbox. Pointing to the still-wrapped gift, I said, "We haven't opened it."

He opened his mouth, but no words came out.

"I'm sorry," I said. Regret settled in my chest.

The doorbell rang. I handed the baby to Tom and opened the door. Marcus stood on the front porch shaking his head.

I held up my hand. "Don't even start with me."

He pinched his lips together and followed me into the living room. I pointed to the box and held out the card. He slipped on gloves, opened an oversized, zippered plastic bag, and stuck both items inside.

"Your fingerprints are already on file, so we can rule them out." He zipped the bag shut. "I'll be in touch."

He turned on his heel and left. I closed the door behind him and leaned my forehead on the cool windowpane. My investigations, my meddling had threatened my family. Who knew what the box contained? I drew a deep breath, exhaled, and returned to the living room. The baby napped on Tom's chest. My daughter was nowhere in sight.

"Where is Chloe?" I sat on the other end of the couch.

"In the bathroom." Tom's jaw worked, the muscles flinching. "Who is this person threatening my family?"

I LEFT AFTER MARCUS. I didn't want to stay and be a danger to them. Let that person follow me, as long as it kept them away from my daughter, son-in-law, and grandson.

I crossed back into Pensacola, pulled into a parking lot, and texted Cynthia.

All done?

She texted back a thumbs-up emoji. She wasn't outside when I parked, so I waited at one of the picnic tables in the front yard. Birds called to each other. Spanish moss swayed from the live oaks, and a soft breeze cooled my brow. My heartbeat slowed. My shoulders lowered. I rubbed the back of my neck and blinked back tears.

No more crying, remember?

The front door slammed, startling me. I looked up to find Harry approaching.

He sat across from me and tilted his head, eyebrows narrowed. "Are you all right, Peg? You look upset."

I took in his charming expression and appreciated the flash of dimple. "Long day."

"I'm sorry." He patted my arm. "Your daughter is very smart."

Music to a mother's ears. "Thank you. She was excited to come help."

He smiled.

Gracious woman. Look anywhere but his dimple. I tucked my hands under my thighs. "Um, what did y'all do today?"

He stood and held out his hand. "Come see."

I followed him but kept my hands to myself. He tapped a code on the door to let us in.

"Top secret stuff?"

"It's more that we have so much research equipment here. When we're open, we override the lock, but on days like today, it's automatic."

"Gotcha."

We entered the bright, cheerful lobby, and I waved to Karla. She raised her eyebrows but didn't say hello. He pointed out brochures and static displays that encouraged visitors to be hands-on as they learned about the birds at the center. He kept touching my arm to show how a display worked or pointing out a specific item. I'd seen most of this when our group toured the place, but I allowed him to be my guide again.

"Come with me," he said after a few minutes.

I followed him toward an office. He used a key to unlock the door and ushered me inside. I stopped and stared.

Thick dark curtains covering the two windows, plus brown-paneled walls, made the space feel closed in. Cave-like. Every available wall held some kind of bird or bird part. Stuffed birds hung on the walls, and several dangled overhead. Bird beaks and feet sat on floating shelves. Mason jars held unidentifiable objects. Feathers were perched everywhere and tucked behind displays. A musty, rank smell permeated the room.

"Interesting decor." I resisted the urge to plug my nose.

"Thanks." Harry closed the door and flipped the lock. He

shoved his hands in his pockets and rocked back on his heels, surveying the office. "It's my favorite room."

I turned to see if he was being sarcastic, but he was relaxed and comfortable. The hair on the back of my neck rose.

"Do you work here often? In Pensacola, I mean. You said you were here for a short time, but your office is very … personalized." I rubbed my arms to cover the shiver running through me.

He sat at the desk and leaned back in his chair. "I come every few months. I've been working here on and off for years. We're researching a specific bird. One that might die out if we don't help."

"Oh?" No other words would come.

"Yes. Would you like to find out more?" He stood and gestured to another door.

"Um, not today. Thanks."

He ducked his head and peered into my eyes. "Are you all right, Peg?" He stepped closer and touched my shoulder. "You seem frightened."

"No, I'm good." My heart skittered. I pulled back from his hand and was about to ask to leave when someone knocked.

"Who is it?" Harry barked without turning around. He held my gaze.

"Me, Dr. Harry. I think my mom is here."

I whooshed out a breath at Cynthia's voice. "Yeah, I gotta go. We … we have to do some stuff," I stammered and raised my voice, "I'm in here, Cynth."

"Okay, Peg." Resignation filled his face, but he unlocked and opened the door, followed me out, and pulled it closed until it latched.

I rushed to Cynthia. "Hi, honey. You ready?" I tugged her toward the front door.

"You okay?"

"We need to leave," I hissed.

She pursed her lips and turned. "Bye, Dr. Harry. I'll see you Thursday?"

"Perfect. Bye, Peg."

I raised my hand without turning around. I opened the door, and it slammed shut behind us. Cynthia pulled me to a stop.

"Mom?"

"I don't ... I don't know, honey. He's so ... peculiar. He kept saying my name and touching my arm." My whole body trembled. I fished the car keys out of my purse and handed them to her. "Can you drive?"

After I buckled up, I shoved my shaking hands under my thighs. Cynthia started the car and backed out.

"Tell me what's going on."

I filled her in on what happened at Chloe's and then described Harry's office. "Have you been in it?"

"No. He gave me a brief tour of the place, but not that room. Sounds a little Norman Batesish.

I agreed. Dr. Harry was a mystery. His office gave me the heebie-jeebies. Sure, he had a cute dimple and liked birds, but something about him didn't ring true. Could I depend on my feelings? My gut? I didn't think that was the best way to go. I liked solving mysteries, but Harry was beyond my limited abilities.

Chapter 11

The vibes I picked up in Harry's office wouldn't leave. At times, he seemed almost normal. Then he'd invade my personal space or offer to show me a locked room. I didn't like it, but it sounded silly when I said it aloud. Like Marcus said, it wasn't a crime to be different.

Shortie hadn't been by in over a week. He'd purchased an old Mustang and was deep into tearing it down before fixing it up. I listened when he called, contributed a few "Yeah" and "Uh-huh" comments, and told him to come see me whenever possible. Another man in my life that I couldn't figure out.

On Thursday, Cynthia used my car to drive to work. I wrote a blog post, checked stats on the blog's dashboard, and called Lauree.

"What are you up to today?" I said when she answered.

"I'm taking the kids to the beach. Want to go?"

The beach sounded perfect. A great escape from my house and my concerns about Harry, Shortie, and the unknown-caller-slash-gift-giver.

"Yes," I said. "I'll be over in a few minutes."

June in Northwest Florida could be sunny and warm,

blazing hot and humid, or chilly and overcast. It was also the start of hurricane season, but we had the perfect day with temperatures in the mid-eighties and a soft breeze. We spread a blanket and weighed it down with the cooler and our flip-flops while the twins ran into the surf. They played at the water's edge, letting their feet get sucked into the sand while Lauree and I sat on the blanket and chatted.

I filled her in on my life and finished with my feelings about Harry.

She nodded and responded, "Hmm," but I could tell she wasn't following my story.

I paused. "You okay?"

"I have to tell you something." She picked at her shorts and avoided my eyes.

"What?"

She didn't speak right away.

I leaned over and patted her hand. "Tell me." Everything in the past few months had been about me. My chaotic life had impacted her. Was that what she wanted to talk about?

She started to speak several times and then blurted, "I found a lump."

At her words, the world stopped turning. I opened my mouth but couldn't speak. Nothing came to mind. I scooted closer and wrapped my arms around her. She sobbed out her fears and worries. I kept an eye on the kids, waving when they turned to see if we were watching.

After several minutes, she sat up and used a beach towel to dry her eyes and nose.

"I don't know what to say," I said.

She grimaced. "It's okay."

"Have you gone to the doctor?"

"Yes." Her nose, plugged from crying, made it sound like "Yeth."

"Mammo? Ultrasound?" Ten years ago, I found a small jellybean-type lump and had both tests. I had a cyst, and it went away. Her body language told me this was different.

She nodded.

I brushed the hair off her face and lifted her chin. "Lauree?"

She looked up. Grief and pain covered her normally cheerful, perky expression. "It's bad, Peg."

My first instinct, first thought—and I'm not proud of it—was what would happen to me? This woman, my best friend, was the reason I survived Zack's death. She and John helped me raise my kids. She stepped in at every opportunity when I wasn't emotionally able to. She was the one I called with my problems. She had the answers. Lauree knew me better than I knew myself.

I forced my problems out of the way. "I'm here. Whatever you need."

Lauree's news cast a giant shadow over the rest of our time at the beach. I forced myself to smile and cheer at the twins as they paddled in the mild surf. I shoved aside all the "What-ifs" and "Oh, my" thoughts bombarding my mind. She had been my strength all these years. I would do the same for her. She asked me not to tell anyone else until she and John talked to the kids.

When I got home, I headed for my room, prepared for a long shower and a good cry. My phone rang, temporarily interrupting my plans.

"Hello," I said, hoping this would be a quick call.

"The Center is planning a fundraiser, Mom. Do you want to contribute to the silent auction?" Cynthia asked.

I stuffed my pain about Lauree and switched gears to listen to my daughter. "Um, I think so. When is it?"

"It's planned for Saturday after next, and we'll have a costume party, the auction, and door prizes. It should be a lot of fun."

"Short notice to plan a party."

"Kurt and Gabby have done some work already. I get to help." Her excitement came through the line. "Dr. Harry invited all the birders too."

"Okay, I'll let them know."

I texted the birding group with the fundraiser date and time, reminded them to wear a costume, and asked for silent auction items to be donated.

"What kind of costume do you wear to a party in Florida in the middle of June?" Hazel asked when I told her.

"Good question. Something comfortable and light. What do we have here we can use?"

She rifled through her room and brought out binoculars and a sun hat. "We can go as birders."

We drove to a nearby thrift shop and found two multi-pocket vests similar to Owen's. We shoved pens and pads of paper in them and looped the binoculars around our necks.

"Ta-da." I threw up my arms.

Roscoe screeched, "Ta-da!" and CB barked.

The day of the party dawned rainy and in the low seventies, but the rain tapered off before we left the house. Hazel, Cynthia, and I rode together. When we arrived, cars were jammed into the parking lot, and we were forced to park on the road.

"This looks promising," Hazel said. "Lots of people here."

Lights twinkled in the trees, and frogs and crickets serenaded us. As the sun set, the sky burned in blues and pinks.

"You couldn't ask for a more perfect night for a fundraiser." I hooked my arms through theirs.

The building's interior lights were out. Cynthia led us around to the back. "We decided to do it outside. Dr. Harry didn't want anyone inside except to use the bathrooms."

I didn't want to be inside. At least, not in his office. How would tonight go—would he be normal Harry or creepy Harry?

Several pelicans tracked our movements from their perch on the bank across Bayou Chico. The crowd enjoyed hors d'oeuvres, and on the deck, we found a small bar. The bartender passed out water bottles and mini cans of soda. A young lady wove through the group with a platter of finger food. I grabbed a stuffed mushroom and popped it into my mouth.

"Yum. I want another of those." I snatched one as she walked off.

Karla lurked in the corner, no costume on, her purse clutched to her belly. I stepped forward to tell her hello when Cynthia touched my arm.

"Shortie is here, Mom." Cynthia pointed.

Butterflies went to work in my stomach. It had been so long since I had seen him, and I missed him. I chuckled at his costume—he was dressed like a pirate, complete with the eye patch and hook on his hand. He hugged us all and kissed my temple. "Original outfit, Peg."

"Thanks." I squeezed his hand, thankful to spend the evening with him.

Dr. Harry approached, and my mouth went dry. He also wore a pirate costume, although his looked like the real thing.

"Dr. Harry Morrison," he said, sticking out his non-hook hand to Shortie.

Shortie shook his hand, using added effort to squeeze it, the muscles in his arm flexing. I slid my arm around his waist.

"Let's go eat," I said, attempting to break the competition between the two men.

"Yes, you two go find some refreshments and check out our silent auction." Harry saluted us with his hook and walked away.

"Smarmy," Shortie muttered.

"What?"

"Nothing. Let's eat."

We signed up under several auction items. I had donated a picture of the desert someone had gifted me, and there was a wide assortment of things to bid on. Kurt and his stepsister handed out door prize tickets. Cynthia had introduced the two of them to us when we first arrived.

Kurt—tall, slender, and cute in a surfer-boy way, lit up when he saw my daughter. Gabby had dark brown eyes and bleached blonde hair with a startling streak of neon green on one side. A beautiful necklace encircled her tanned neck, but Karla pulled her away before I had a chance to ask her about it.

When the sun went down, Cynthia and Gabby lit Tiki torches. Those and strings of white twinkle lights around the deck and gazebo kept the encroaching summer night away. Harry stood on a chair and whistled. Everyone looked his way, and he waved us all closer. "I hope you're having fun tonight."

The crowd cheered. So far, Cynthia had won a stuffed flamingo and Hazel a pelican pin from the door prizes.

"We'll announce the silent auction winners soon. But first, the costume contest." He surveyed the people near him. "Some of you have outdone yourselves." He caught my eye, then glared at Shortie. "Others, not so much."

Shortie muttered under his breath.

Gabby waved all the people wearing costumes to line up along the bank of Bayou Chico. "Here you go." She positioned people and moved some around. "Dr. Harry?"

He stepped down from the deck and walked along the line of contestants, joking with them as he went along. Shortie and I were the last in line, and when he got to me, he reached out and squeezed my shoulder. He ignored Shortie.

I pinched my lips together. Shortie's irritation hung between us, and I chanced a look at him. His clenched jaw told the story. I leaned over. "Sorry."

He gave a sharp nod.

Harry turned and walked back to the beginning of the line. He raised his hand above each person as he made his way through the contestants. Cheers rang out, some louder than others. He stopped in front of Shortie, glared, and raised his hooked hand over his head. I cheered and whistled. As Harry brought his hook down, he clipped Shortie's shoulder hard enough to knock him off balance. He lost his footing and tripped backward, landing in the bayou with a splash.

Everyone froze. The pelicans startled and took flight. The frogs and crickets quieted. Shortie stood up, minus the eye patch and hook, and sloshed ashore. Harry stepped back at the look in Shortie's eyes.

"So sorry, buddy." Harry took another step away.

Shortie stood beside me, raking his hair from his face and sluicing water from his eyes. "No problem, *buddy*." His clipped words, body language, and dark eyes screamed anger.

I slipped my hand into his. "Let's let you clean up."

"Nah. Let's stay and see who won," he said through gritted teeth.

Gabby spoke up, her voice shaky, "And the winner is ... Terry Johnson!"

Harry approached the first person in line and congratulated her. We all clapped, Shortie and I with less enthusiasm.

I tugged him toward the front of the building. "I can't believe what he did."

He pulled me to a stop. "Peg, he did it on purpose."

"I know." I did. Harry shoved Shortie hard and with purpose.

He tipped up my chin, a question in his eyes. "Are you interested in him?"

"Nope, not at all." Whatever I wasn't sure of, this showed me one thing. I was not interested in Harry. "No way, no how."

Shortie studied my face, then leaned in for a kiss. My concerns and my questions melted away. I wrapped my arms around him. We stood in a soggy embrace until a bird screeched.

I jumped. "The front door should be unlocked. You can dry off in the men's room. Cynthia said Harry didn't want anyone in his office, but we can use the bathrooms."

I waited in the lobby while he dried off. The air conditioning clicked on, and Harry's office door moved. I reached out and touched it. It opened a bit, and I hopped back.

Hazel came in the front door. "Peg, is Shortie okay?"

I froze. "He's cleaning up. He's frustrated."

She narrowed her eyes and stepped closer. "The door's open? Is that Harry's office?"

"Mm-hmm."

"Try it again."

I tapped it, and the door swung farther open. Hazel and I exchanged looks.

"What do we do now?" I asked.

Chapter 12

"We go in." She tugged me into the room, closed the door, and flipped on the lights. "You were right. This is an eerie place."

I turned off the light. "We can't have that on. They'll see us. We'll have to use our phone flashlights. Shield it with your hand, though." I clicked on mine and showed her what I meant. I shined it around the room. It looked the same, except ... I stopped, and she ran into me. "Look, Hazel."

She turned her light to my face, blinding me. "What?"

"On the desk." I blinked my eyes several times to remove the imprint from her flashlight. When I could see again, Hazel held the item.

"It's another quetzal feather," she whispered.

"Wow." I ran my finger over it. "How did Harry get this one?"

"He has to be part of this, Peg. We tie him to the Keatons, and we'll solve Roger's murder." She shook the feather in my face.

She might be correct, but I wasn't sure it would be that easy.

"Put it back. Let's keep looking." I scanned the office again. "Harry specializes in studying birds. There must be a good reason he has the feather." I ran my flashlight over the wall where the interior locked door was. This time, though, no light showed. "Wait, I think the other room is open too."

Hazel set the feather on the desk and held the back of my shirt as I approached the doorway. "What do you see?"

I reached behind me and peeled off her fingers. "Quit choking me."

"Sorry." She let go but continued to walk on my heels, her breath hot against my neck.

We entered the interior room, and I shined my light around the walls. The musty odor from Harry's office accompanied an underlying scent of iron.

"What do you see?" Hazel repeated.

I swatted her away. "Back up a little." I shuffled forward another step. "A lot of the same stuff from the other room." More shelving held mason jars with things floating in them. I still didn't want to know what they were. A glitter on a shelf to my right caught my eye. I leaned closer and shined my light on it. Round coins or buttons lay in a pile.

"What are those?" Hazel said.

I rifled through the pieces. "Gold and silver coins, I think. Not sure if they're real."

"What if they're from the shipwreck?" she said, awe in her voice.

"If they are, I want to know why Harry has them." I examined one and stuck it in my pocket.

"You can't steal that."

"I'm not stealing. I want to look at it in a better light." I stepped farther in and kicked something. "Oops."

"What happened?" She peered over my shoulder.

I gritted my teeth. "Close enough? Do you want a piggyback ride?"

She snorted.

I aimed the light at my feet.

"Oh, oh, oh." I backed up. Hazel's feet and mine tangled up, and we tumbled to the floor. Hazel landed on top of me with a grunt.

The door to Harry's office opened, and the overhead light clicked on. I closed my eyes and laid my head back, praying I hadn't seen what I thought I did. The image of a body and a pool of blood burned on the inside of my eyelids.

"What are you two doing in here?" Shortie stood over us, hands on his hips, eyebrows pulled into a deep furrow.

"The door was unlocked." I pushed off of Hazel and struggled to sit.

He leaned over her. "Are you okay?"

She sat up with a shaky smile and wiggled her arms and legs.

I touched her shoulder. "Anything broken?"

"I think I'm all right." She took Shortie's hand and stood. "What happened, Peg? Why did you rush out?"

I got up, closed my eyes, and shivered—the image of what I saw wouldn't disappear. I rubbed my hands up and down my arms. "Kurt. Kurt is in the room. I think he's dead. There's a lot of blood." My words tumbled over each other.

Hazel swung her flashlight into my eyes and screeched, "What?"

"Put that down." I grabbed her cell phone and turned off the light. "You keep blinding me."

"Kurt's in there?" she said. The disbelief in her voice mirrored how I felt.

"Yes. I walked into him." I wanted to run away and hide.

"Where is his body?" Shortie pinched the bridge of his nose.

I gestured toward the other room and followed him to the doorway. He clicked on the light and looked around, me on his heels and Hazel behind me.

He turned. "You've never been in here before?"

"No," I mouthed, unable to push the word past my dry lips.

He moved out of the way, and we saw Kurt lying on his stomach, face turned toward us. Blood pooled under his blond locks. Shortie waved us back. I gagged and broke out in a sweat, head to toe.

"We need to call the police and an ambulance," he said with a grave tone.

I handed him my phone. "Marcus is on speed dial," I choked out.

He called Detective Sharp and reported what I found. Me. I found another dead body. How did this keep happening? The room spun, and I plopped to the ground, head hanging low.

"Peg, are you all right?" Hazel crouched beside me and patted my back. "Come on, take a breath. There you go. Exhale. Breathe in, breathe out." She coached me until the spinning stopped.

"You okay now?" She peered into my eyes.

I nodded, and she helped me up. Shortie put his arm around my shoulders and guided me into the lobby area. He peeked behind the counter, found a chair, and rolled it my way.

"Here, sit."

He didn't have to tell me twice.

"Thank you," I whispered.

"Is Marcus coming?" Hazel asked. She kept a firm grip on my shoulder.

"Yes. Think I need to let everyone at the party know?"

Shortie rubbed the back of his neck. His clothes were still soaking wet, and his shoes squished with every step he took.

Sirens wailed, and flashing lights swirled around the room. We didn't need to inform the partygoers the police were coming. They were here. Shortie stepped outside to meet them. When he returned, he was followed by Marcus, two other police officers, and three EMTs.

"What is going on?" Harry rushed into the building, lip curled and fists clenched. "Why are you in here?" Anger rolled off his body.

"Shortie came in to dry off." I wanted to say, "Duh," seeing as Harry was the reason he fell in the bayou.

Hazel stayed beside me, her hand trembling on my shoulder. I reached up and gripped it.

Marcus moved in front of Harry. "Detective Sharp, sir. Can you tell me what happened? Shortie reported a dead body?"

Harry's face blanched. He stepped back, stumbling over his feet. "What?"

"I found it. It's Kurt. The body, I mean." My words tripped over my tongue.

Someone gasped. Cynthia stood in the doorway, her hands over her mouth. "Mom?"

The police pushed into Harry's office. I stood and pulled my daughter in for a hug.

"Kurt?" she whispered in my ear.

"Mm-hmm." I had to tell her the truth. I had no idea how or when he had died. "Wait." I leaned back and brushed her hair off her face. "He was here tonight. I saw him. When did you see him last?"

She rubbed her eyes. "I talked to him for a few minutes when we first got here. He was busy helping Gabby with door prizes."

I remembered seeing them passing out tickets and calling numbers for the prizes. "You didn't see him again?"

She shook her head.

"Hazel, did you?" I asked.

"No, I never saw him after he handed me my pelican pin." She plopped into the chair I'd vacated.

"Hmm." I turned toward Harry's office. Police swarmed the small room. Harry stood to the side, hands on his head. Anxiety wafted off him, and I assumed he worried what the police would think about his weird collection. I remembered the coin I picked up and patted my pocket to make sure I still had it.

Did Harry know why Kurt died? And where the coins came from? I looked for Marcus, but another gasp at the building's front door brought me up short. Kurt's stepsister, Gabby, entered the room, her neon green streak silhouetted by the outside lights. Her face paled, and she lifted a trembling hand.

"Kurt?" Tears filled her eyes. A couple trickled over and ran down her cheeks. She rushed toward Harry's office, but Cynthia stopped her.

"You can't go inside the room yet." She patted Gabby's back, keeping a firm grip on her. "When did you see him last?"

Gabby jerked away. She crossed her arms and shook her head, mumbling, "It was an accident, it was an accident."

Her words confused me. "What do you mean?"

She stared at me in disbelief. "What?"

"You said it was an accident." It dawned on me that she couldn't see Kurt's body when she first stood in the doorway of the building. I stepped away from her and pulled Cynthia and Hazel with me out the front door.

"What's the matter?" Hazel said.

I stopped in the entranceway to double-check. Nope, you couldn't see past the door of Harry's office. I explained my thoughts to the two of them. They grouped up behind me.

"Do we tell Marcus?" Hazel whispered.

"I think we need to," I said.

Partygoers crowded into the parking lot and asked for information. We were swept up with the group. Police officers took statements and ordered everyone to stay until we were questioned.

After a half hour had passed and we hadn't been interviewed, I turned to Hazel and Cynthia. "Let's go back inside if we can."

We shuffled away from the crowd toward the right and stepped back until we stood under the building's overhang. Someone cleared his throat, and we turned.

"Peg." Marcus stood in the doorway, his dark eyes unreadable in the gloomy night.

Hazel took the lead. "What did you find? Can you tell why Kurt died? How he died?"

Cynthia winced.

"Of course, we don't know yet why he died." Marcus's words were sharp. He coughed and closed his eyes, then drew a deep breath. "Sorry, Hazel."

She nodded her acceptance of his apology.

He stood to the side and waved us into the lobby. "Come on in, and I'll tell you what I can. I have questions for you."

Harry's office door was shut, and crime scene tape spanned from door frame to door frame. My heart sank. I'd seen the tape too many times now. While I waited for Marcus to speak, I counted the deaths—Anna, Sylvia, Roger, and now Kurt. One finger left on my hand. Tears stung my eyes.

Someone found chairs for the three of us, plus Shortie. I sat beside him, and he clasped my cold hand in his. Gabby wasn't anywhere around.

Marcus leaned against the lobby's front desk, arms crossed over his chest, a stern expression on his face. He shook his head and exhaled. "Okay. I don't even know what to say. You guys were present for the last two deaths I've investigated."

Outside, an engine roared, and tires squealed.

"On the flip side, you were at the last two deaths we've been at," I quipped. It wasn't funny, but I was loopy at this point. Nothing made sense, especially another death.

A police officer hurried into the building and spoke to Marcus. Surprise crossed his face, and he barked orders to the officer, "Track down that person now."

"Who?" I asked.

He refocused on us. "Someone left before being questioned. We don't know who."

I counted the people in the room again. "Where's Gabby?"

Chapter 13

She wasn't the only person unaccounted for. No one knew for sure who had attended the fundraiser, but I pointed out that the two people serving drinks and food weren't present. Karla and Gabby couldn't be found. Marcus told Harry to write as many names as he remembered. Some we knew from the costume contest, and many we didn't.

When the medical examiner came, Kurt's death became even more real to me. I hoped he had fallen and hit his head. Head wounds bleed so much. But the arrival of the ME confirmed it was something else.

Cynthia nudged me. "Why is she here?" She pointed to the ME.

"Medical examiners investigate suspicious deaths," Shortie answered.

She wrapped her arms around herself. "I hoped he'd tripped and hit his head."

Her words echoed my thoughts.

"What is a coroner for then? I thought they did all of this." Hazel waved her hand toward Harry's office.

"The coroner is a public officer, and they certify the cause of death." Shortie shrugged. "Two different jobs."

After the EMTs removed Kurt's body, the police let us leave, but Harry called to Cynthia on our way out the door.

"Can you come tomorrow and help me clean up?" Harry stood by his office and waited for her answer.

She grimaced. "Sure, I can."

His question grated on my nerves, but I raised my hand. "I can help too." Shortie winced. I'd explain my reasoning to him when we left.

"Thank you, Peg." Harry nodded, spun on his heel, and strode down the side hall toward the restrooms and the other exit.

Hazel, Shortie, Cynthia, and I headed out the front door for the parking lot. Our cars were the last ones left. I glanced around but didn't see one for Harry.

"What does Harry drive, Cynthia?" I stopped next to the Bug and peered into the darkness.

"No idea. Let's go home, Mom," she said, exhaustion in her voice.

A boat motor roared to life. "That's around back, isn't it?" I hurried past the building to the gazebo and deck area and spotted a small boat pulling away from the shore. Harry sat in the back, holding onto the motor's handle.

"Huh." It occurred to me I didn't know where he lived, but now I knew he could reach his home by boat. I rejoined Hazel, Cynthia, and Shortie and told them what I'd seen.

"I'm tired. We can ask him tomorrow." Cynthia climbed into the back of the Bug.

Shortie stopped me from getting in the car. "What are you up to, Peg?"

"I want to help and look around. I'm not sure I want Cynthia here tomorrow alone with Harry."

He sighed and shook his head. I kissed him goodnight and climbed into the passenger seat. I reached back and patted Cynthia's knee. "I'm so sorry, honey. I know you liked Kurt."

She swiped her eyes. "Who killed him? And why? I don't understand any of this."

Hazel started the car and pulled out of the parking lot. "None of this makes sense. Now we have two quetzal feathers, gold and silver coins, and two dead people."

"Hazel? We have one feather and one coin," I said.

She arched a brow, seeming amused at my question. "I might have pocketed the other feather and some more coins." When I didn't respond, she frowned. "Come on now, you'd have done the same if you'd thought of it."

"What are you two talking about?" Cynthia asked.

I filled her in on our other discoveries in Harry's offices. Hazel pulled the feather from an inside vest pocket and handed it to me. I twirled it, its colors flashing in the passing streetlights.

"And the rest, please." I held out my hand. She rummaged in another pocket and pulled out six coins. I added mine to her pile and handed them back to Cynthia. "We think these are from the caravel that was discovered."

She separated the coins. "Four gold and three silver. How can we find out for sure where these came from?"

We were silent for several minutes.

"I have a thought," Hazel said. She turned, her eyes sparkling. "Owen. He's our resident historian. If he doesn't know, he might have connections."

Cynthia patted her shoulder. "Good idea, Grandma. And you'll get to spend some time with him."

Hazel wiggled her eyebrows. "Smart girl. I like that. I'll call him tomorrow."

$\sim$

I'D PUSHED Lauree's news from my mind for the last two days, but when I went to bed, her diagnosis consumed my thoughts. She hadn't told me much except it was bad. I made a mental note to check on her in the morning and see how I could help. The idea of my best friend facing such a fight brought tears to my eyes. Lauree might be a strong person, but I also recognized how insidious cancer could be. I forced my thoughts to the positive and reminded myself how many strides they'd made in research and in curing breast cancer. Also, that God knew all about this. He was in charge, and I trusted Him. I whispered prayers for her as I drifted off to sleep.

The next morning, I texted her and asked when we could get together to chat. She suggested lunch on Monday after she had some tests done. I sent her a thumbs-up, torn between wanting to know the details and preferring to stick my head in the sand and pretend none of it was true. I didn't try to imagine how she felt.

After breakfast, Hazel called Owen and explained what we found. "Can you take a look at the coins? You can come here, or I'll come over."

Cynthia made kissing sounds, and Hazel glared at her.

"Stop," she hissed. Into her cell, she said, "No, not you, Owen. Cynthia is making noises." She wrinkled her nose at her granddaughter.

Cynthia laughed and said, "Mom, I'm heading to the Center. Want to come?"

I held up a finger, waiting to hear when Hazel planned to go to Owen's. I wanted to be at the Center and investigate, but I also wanted to find out what Owen knew about the coins.

Hazel finished her conversation and hung up. "I'm going to his house this afternoon around four."

Perfect. That fit my schedule. "I'll be back in time to go with you."

Her shoulders slumped, and I laughed.

"I don't think he'll make a move today, Hazel."

She stuck out her tongue at me and waved Cynthia and me out of the house. We climbed into my car, Cynthia in the driver's seat.

"What are you looking for today?" she asked.

I buckled up as she backed out of the driveway. "I'm not sure. I'd love to peek into his inside office and see if he has more treasures from the caravel. If he had the coins, I imagine he has other items."

I'd have to get a key to his main office first and then sneak inside. I still hadn't figured him out. He loved birds, obviously, and although I thought his collection was different, that didn't make him a bad guy. But how did he get his hands on the coins? And the quetzal feather?

"So, we have two murders, another feather, and coins," I said.

She groaned. "I don't understand how you deal with all this, Mom. It's so ..." She shook her head.

"I'm sorry, honey. It is a lot. I'm thinking aloud. Remember when you researched quetzals? These feathers both come from resplendent quetzals. It might be one bird or two. One went missing from Guatemala. I'm trying to make connections. We never came up with a list of suspects, did we?"

"No. But you mentioned Estelle Keaton."

"Yes. She was the mastermind, like Grandma said. I don't think she gets her hands dirty in any of this. If she's behind her husband and Kurt's deaths, she'd use another person." It wasn't Neil Braden this time. He was in prison for Sylvia and Anna's murders.

"Who do you think it is then?" She pulled into the Center's parking lot and turned off the car.

"I'm not sure. Let's talk to Owen this afternoon, and then we'll make a list. Right now, too many ideas are swirling in my mind."

We entered the building, and I noticed the police crime tape had been removed.

"Dr. Harry?" Cynthia called.

Rustling sounded from down the hall.

"What's back there?" I asked.

"Storage rooms. Two of them. I haven't been in them, though."

I tucked the information in the back of my mind. They would be good places to search. "Let's see if he's in one of them."

We passed the bathrooms. Farther down were two doors, one on each side of the hall.

"Harry? Are you here?" I called.

More noises came before the door on the right opened. He poked his head out. "I'll be right out." He slammed the door shut, and the lock clicked.

Cynthia and I looked at each other.

"I wonder what he's doing." I kept my voice low.

She made a face and shook her head. "What if he has more quetzals?"

She had a point. The Center was all about birds. Harry might be involved with Estelle and the missing quetzals. It felt like less of a stretch than before, and I wanted to find out everything. I needed a way into the locked room.

Harry exited the storage room and locked the door behind him, slipping the key into his pants pocket. He rubbed his hands together and flashed a smile, the dimple on his cheek prominent.

"You two ready to work?"

"Sure. Where do you want us to start?" I asked.

"I have someone coming to clean the … blood. It needs a professional cleaner." He stared at his feet. "I can't believe Kurt is gone."

I nodded. "It's so surreal." I gestured to the storage room opposite the one he'd been in. "Do you have cleaning supplies? We can start outside. Pick up the trash and all and put the chairs back where they go."

He opened the door—unlocked, I noticed—and flipped on the light. "What you need should be in here. If you clean out back, I can wait for the cleaner and work on my office."

Cynthia and I found trash bags and a broom and headed out the side door. When I saw the mess, I groaned. "This will take a while."

Cynthia fluffed open a trash bag and held it out to me. "I'll hold this, and you can toss things in."

We made our way around the deck area, the gazebo, and the bayou, filling four bags with plastic serving dishes, plates, napkins, and water bottles. Some trash had blown into the water. I checked the storage room for something to fish it out with, but nothing looked like it would work. I tugged on the other door without luck.

"Dr. Harry?" I called.

He emerged from his office. "Yes?"

"What can we use for the trash in the water? I looked in the storage room, but we need a net. I tried the other room, and the door is locked."

"Yes, you don't need to go in there. It's my, um, extra office."

How many offices did one man need? If he came to Pensacola now and then for research, why more than one? His comment raised my suspicions.

"Where do you live when you're not in Pensacola?"

He gestured behind him. "I have a boat at the marina."

"No, I mean when you're not here." Was he being intentionally obtuse?

He leaned against the door frame and crossed his arms over his chest. "Wherever my boat and the birds take me."

I decided to take a chance. "We found a quetzal feather on your desk last night. Do you study quetzals? Have you been to Mexico?"

His face turned to stone. He stood up straight, arms down, fists clenched. He stepped toward me, and I glimpsed something unsettling in his eyes. "Now, why would you ask that, Peg?"

Chapter 14

"**I**'m curious." I shrugged, trying to appear casual. "We ... we found the other quetzal feather out at Fort Pickens, remember? Cynthia showed it to you?" I backed up a step, ready to turn and run. His expression scared me.

He stood stock still, and then his demeanor changed. It was the oddest thing I'd ever seen. His shoulders relaxed, fists unclenched, and a crooked grin lit up his face. "Oh, yes, I remember."

I waited for him to say more, but he stared at me with a blank look.

"Okay, well, a net? Do you have one?" Whatever happened to him just now, I wanted to leave. He kept reinforcing my opinion of him as an odd duck.

"Sure, hang on." He darted into his office and returned with a net on a long pole. "Will this help?"

"Yes, perfect." I took it and hurried down the hall and out the door. A prickling sensation ran through my body. I wasn't sure how much more I could take of Dr. Harry.

"Here." I passed the pole to Cynthia. I wrapped my arms around myself when she took it.

"You okay?"

I nodded and explained how Harry had been and how he'd changed.

Cynthia cocked an eyebrow. "Hmm. Let's finish here, and then we'll look around. Maybe we can figure all this out."

We scooped most of the trash from the bayou but couldn't reach all of it. Harry's johnboat rested on the bank nearby, so I shoved it into the water, climbed in, and started the motor. Cynthia joined me, and we made a slow circle in our area of the bayou, retrieving the rest of the garbage from the previous night.

"Harry told me he has a bigger boat. He lives on it at a marina," I said.

Cynthia tied the trash bag shut and swiped sweat from her face with the back of her hand. "And?"

"Let's run down the bayou. Think we can find it?" I left the Center's area and motored out into Bayou Chico.

Her eyes narrowed. "Mom, it's too far. We don't know for sure which marina he's at or what kind of boat he has. We'll be gone too long."

She was right. I estimated it would be close to an hour to the bay and back. Harry would wonder where we were—no telling how he'd act. Not to mention how many marinas existed in and around the Pensacola area.

"Okay, we'll go back." I would drive around later and check things out. Narrowing down which marina he lived at would be tricky. They weren't like hotels, where I could call and ask if he docked there.

I steered the boat back to shore and cut the motor. We gathered all the trash bags and slung them in the dumpster. I opened the side door and headed for the ladies' restroom to wash my hands. As we passed Harry's "extra" office, I noticed the door stood ajar. I grabbed Cynthia's arm and pulled her to a stop. "Look."

She tapped the door, and it swung open. A sense of déjà vu swept over me. Last time I entered an open door, I found Kurt. Dead.

Anxiety pooled in my stomach. "I'm not so sure about this."

She ignored me, reached into the room, and flipped the light switch. "You stay out here. I'll take a look around."

Where was my frightened daughter from the night before? I wouldn't wait in the hall and send her inside the room alone. I leaned the net against the door frame, gripped her shoulder, and followed her.

"Dr. Harry?" she whispered.

No answer and no noise.

"Where do you think he is?" I asked in a quiet voice. My heartbeat pulsed in my ears and sounded loud in the silence.

She shrugged and stepped farther into the room. I let go of her and surveyed the space. Harry's office was strange, and the interior one where Kurt died was much like it. This one had empty walls, and boards covered the lone window. Two large metal desks were pushed together in the middle of the room, and three small cages sat on them. We stepped closer. Each cage held two or three tiny, pale-blue eggs.

"What is he doing with those?" I bent over for a better look.

Cynthia took out her phone and snapped a picture. She searched the internet for a matching image. She held her cell out to me, her hand shaking. "Mom, I think these are quetzal eggs."

He had to have more than two birds if he had this many eggs.

We hurried out of the office and pulled the door tight. I had no idea how or why he had the quetzal eggs. None of this made sense. He had to be involved with Estelle Keaton. Cynthia and I hurried up the hall, calling for Harry.

We reached the lobby, and he stepped from behind the desk. "Here I am. What do you need?"

"We finished outside. We're about to leave." I chewed on the inside of my cheek and attempted to keep my face neutral and my voice steady. I avoided his eyes. Somehow, in some way, Harry was involved with the quetzals. Meaning he knew the Keatons. I needed to connect those dots, but not here at the Center.

His cheerful expression fell, and his shoulders slumped. "I thought you would stay longer. Karla is leaving, and I'm still waiting on the cleaners."

The woman gathered her purse and touched Harry's arm. "I'll see you tomorrow, Doc." She winked at him, gave me the stink-eye, and waltzed out the door.

"I can stay a while, Dr. Harry," Cynthia said.

Karla left, and I tried to figure out why she didn't like me. Cynthia's words penetrated my brain. "How will you get home?" Did I want her here alone with him?

"I can bring her home." Harry stepped forward. "No problem."

It concerned me to leave Cynthia with him. "You're sure?" I asked my daughter.

"Go on, Mom. You and Grandma need to meet with Mr. Owen, remember?"

"Yes." I turned my back to Harry and gave her a questioning look. She responded with a slight nod. "Okay, I'm leaving. Call me if you end up needing a ride." I held my fingers to my ear like I was making a phone call.

Harry opened the front door. "We'll be fine." He let the door smack closed behind me, and I jumped.

I took my cell phone out of my purse and texted Cynthia

Be careful!

No answer and no three little dots.

A headache wove its way up my neck and across my forehead.

When I pulled up to my house, Hazel sat on the front porch rocker, her purse in her lap. I parked at the curb, opened the passenger window, and hollered, "You ready?"

She nodded and made her way up the lawn. "I already put CB inside and locked the door." She huffed a few times and tried to catch her breath. "Your yard is so steep."

My eye twitched. She mentioned the yard and driveway a lot.

"Where is Cynthia?" she asked as she buckled up.

"She volunteered to stay at the Center and help more. Guess what we found?" I filled her in on the quetzal eggs.

"Amazing. So now we have to find out how Dr. Harry knows Estelle."

"Yes, I had the same thought. If he does, we need to figure out where Estelle is."

Hazel directed me to Owen's, who lived near the University of West Florida in a small, pale-blue bungalow-style home. White columns supported a deep front porch, complete with several white wicker rockers. His lawn glistened a brilliant green as if it had just been watered. We parked, and he came out the front door and joined us beside the car.

"It's a beautiful day. Let's go out back and sit by the pond," he said.

We followed him around the side of the house to a group of four sling-backed chairs and a wrought-iron coffee table. We sat, admiring the area and enjoying the slight breeze.

"This is so peaceful." Hazel patted Owen's arm. What a lovely place."

"My wife and I lived here for years. After she died, I stayed. The house is the right size for me, and the neighbors are all friendly." He turned to me. "What did you want to talk about?"

Hazel opened her purse and removed the two quetzal feathers and seven coins. She reminded him that Cynthia found the first feather and explained where we discovered the other items.

Owen accepted them from her, placed the bird feathers in his lap, and examined the coins. He looked at each one, his forehead wrinkled in concern. "I have a friend we can ask about these." He handed them all back to Hazel.

"Who?" I asked.

"Margaret Turnball. She helped in the discovery of the other DeLuna ships. It seems these might be from one of those."

"Or the most recent one found," I said. "The 'rogue' ship." I made air quotes.

He nodded and rose from his chair. "Follow me."

We traipsed across his lawn and behind two other houses before climbing three steps to a back screened-in porch. Owen opened the screen door and knocked on the house's back door.

He turned to us. "I've known Maggie for years. She volunteers at the high school once a week, but I think she's home today." He knocked again, wiggled the doorknob, turned it, and stuck his head in. "Maggie? Dr. Turnball? Are you home?"

"Owen? Is that you?" A loud voice preceded a petite woman with a halo of fluffy, white hair. She wore large, round, black glasses, a pale blue shirt with Native American designs, silver cuff bracelets, and a chunky blue stone necklace.

"She's unique," Hazel whispered.

Here was a woman with history, someone comfortable in

her own skin, willing to wear whatever she wanted and get away with it. I admired her.

Owen introduced us and said we had some coins to show her. Maggie—she asked us to call her that—ushered us into her house and to the front room.

"Have a seat. Sweet tea, coffee, or water?" She had a brisk, authoritative manner.

We placed our orders, and I jumped up to help.

"I'm fine, young lady." She waved me away.

I stifled my grin. "My momma taught me manners, though." I followed her into her kitchen.

Her dark brown eyes sparkled, and her lips twitched. She filled a glass with ice and sweet tea and passed it to me. "You can carry yours."

"Thank you." I waited while she got the other drinks. "Your kitchen is very eclectic."

"Like me, you mean."

I smiled. "You said it, not me. I love the colors and décor."

"Thank you." She surveyed the room. "Each item has a story. In my younger days, I traveled quite a bit."

I could tell. Framed and unframed pictures hung beside African masks and old-fashioned eyeglasses, with other signs and knickknacks in between. I leaned in for a closer look at one photo. "Is that Owen?"

"Yes, Dr. Walters has been part of two of the archeological teams I led." She handed me another glass and picked up a box of cookies. I followed her to the sitting room, where we passed out drinks, and she offered each of us a treat.

"Have you been in her kitchen?" I asked Owen. "She has a picture of you in there."

"Dr. Walters comes over every week when we play cards." Maggie settled into an armchair and sipped her tea. "Now, what did you want to know about your discoveries?"

Chapter 15

Owen didn't have all the up-to-date information, and Maggie knew nothing. All the things that happened, from the dead bodies last fall up to our discovery of the coins at the Center, flashed through my mind. Where to start?

Hazel jumped right in. "We found seven coins, and we want to confirm what they are and where they're from. Can you help us?"

Good job, Hazel. Straightforward and concise. I nibbled on a chocolate chip cookie, content to let her take the lead.

"Where did you find them?" Maggie asked.

My mother-in-law turned to me. "I'll let Peg tell you the details."

Throwing me under the bus, I see. I narrowed my eyes at her and turned to Maggie. "Some of this is speculation, but we found them in an office at a local business."

"That's speculation?" She tipped her head, her fluffy hair bouncing with the movement.

"No, no. Sorry." I finished my cookie and wiped my sweaty palms on my capris. "It's a long story. Lots of stuff ..." I waved my hand. I didn't want to go into the background leading us to this moment. "What kind of coins are these, and could they be from the ship that was just discovered?"

Maggie sat back in her chair, a strange expression on her face. After a moment, she held out her hand, and Hazel passed her a small, zippered plastic bag. Maggie opened the baggie and withdrew one coin. She ran her finger over it, turned it over, and peered at the details. She put it down and fished out the others. She leaned forward and placed them on the coffee table in two separate piles—four gold coins and three silver.

She gestured to the piles and glanced at Owen. "Do you remember what we heard?"

He nodded, concern flashing in his eyes.

Maggie scooped up the coins, stuck them in the baggie, zipped it closed, and handed it back to Hazel. "I don't think I can help you." Her lips thinned.

Hazel and I exchanged glances. Why were we here, then? Owen said Maggie could identify what we had found. What was up with these two? I never pegged Owen as anything but honest and trustworthy, but he was holding back something.

"Okay, what's up?" I looked between the two of them. "Owen, you knew these coins might be from the caravel they discovered. Maggie, are you worried about us having them? What's going on here?"

Maggie sat back and drew a deep breath. "I worked two of the three de Luna wrecks. We never found items like these." She fiddled with her necklace. "I heard rumors during my time on the ships."

"Rumors?" Hazel asked.

"She came to me," Owen jumped in, his voice troubled. "She knew my background in history, of course, and she worried about the truth of the stories."

Maggie scooted forward and clutched her glass of sweet

tea. Her hand shook as she raised it. "I did. If they were true, we were all at risk."

"What kind of risk?" I tried to move the conversation along.

Maggie set down her tea and removed her glasses, wiping them on her shirt. "People that find coins in wreckage from that ship ... well, they will die. Or be killed." Fear flitted across her face. "Have there been any deaths since you found these?"

I gulped. Owen and Hazel turned to me. I held up two fingers.

"Two?" Maggie's shrill voice sent goosebumps up my arms.

"Yes," I whispered. "We found Roger Keaton's body."

"I did." Hazel raised her hand. "I mean, I found him. I didn't kill him." She stammered over her words.

Maggie's kind brown eyes hardened. "Who else died?"

"I stumbled into the body of one of the employees at the Bird Rescue and Care Center. Kurt. I don't know his last name. I found him dead in the same room where we found these coins."

Maggie's eyebrows rose. She stood and gestured for us to get up. "Why would you bring them here, Owen? You know better. Now I'm at risk too. You need to leave. Now. Take those things with you." She flapped her hand at the baggie.

We followed Owen out the front door, and Maggie slammed it behind us. I turned to Owen. "You know more. Much more than a rumor."

He grimaced. "Let's go to my house." He turned on the walkway to his front door, let us in, and waved toward a formal sitting room. "Have a seat. I'll be right back."

"I don't believe in curses," Hazel whispered as we sat on a floral-patterned crushed velvet loveseat. "Do you think that's what Maggie means? That the coins are cursed and people die when they find them?"

I didn't know what was happening, but I didn't believe in curses, either. Owen and Maggie were both well-educated professors. Yet they fell for the rumors.

Owen entered the room, a large, ornate book in his hands. He sat in a wingback armchair covered in the same material as the loveseat and patted the book's cover. "This will help explain what Maggie said. There is speculation—" He narrowed his eyes. "But we don't believe the coins are cursed. At least, I don't. I think someone spread the story because they knew they were in the wreckage. If people believe they might die or be killed, then no one would explore the ship."

That made sense. "Who started the rumors?" I asked.

He shrugged. "People have talked about them for a few years."

I didn't understand. The other de Luna ships were discovered a number of years ago.

Owen opened the book, flipped through the pages, and turned it toward us.

"This is a drawing of de Luna's fleet. See that little ship tucked in the middle in the back? That's what they found the other day." He ran his fingers down the page, leaned in, and read, "The Caravel Santa Maria joined Tristan de Luna's ships as they sailed from Mexico up the Gulf toward Pensacola. It's believed the caravel carried gold and silver coins, and maybe gems, and that a hurricane destroyed it."

He read more to himself and glanced up. "There's nothing here about a rumor or curse. That wasn't mentioned until the de Luna's wrecks were discovered." He tapped the book. "Someone knows what the Santa Maria had on board."

And someone didn't want anyone else to know.

"How would people find out about the caravel before someone discovered it? What it held, I mean?" Hazel followed me into my house. "Is there a club for people interested in shipwrecks?"

I set my purse on the island. "Look for information on archaeological websites." My mother-in-law might be in her late sixties, but she understood technology as well as my kids.

She retrieved her laptop, set it on the dining table, and turned it on. "I'll take CB out to potty. Then I'll see what I can find." She clicked her tongue, and CB bounced up and trotted after her.

I checked my phone while they were outside, but Cynthia hadn't messaged or called. I would text her if I didn't hear from her in a few more minutes.

Carter's bedroom door opened. He emerged with a loud yawn.

"Good nap?" I grinned. He looked like he did as a toddler. Only taller.

He rubbed his eyes, yawned again, and stretched. "I fell asleep reading. What's for dinner?"

Good question. I opened the refrigerator and looked through the few items inside. Time for a trip to the grocery store. "How about pancakes?"

"Yum. I'm gonna shower."

I mixed the pancake batter, adding pecans and fresh blueberries. While the griddle heated, Hazel and CB came inside. She tapped on her laptop and summarized what she'd learned.

"I see a few older news reports. Some about UWF students assisting with the de Luna shipwrecks." She squinted and leaned toward her laptop. "Okay, here is a similar picture to what Owen showed us. It has the caravel near the back of the group of ships. Says it is a caravel named Santa Maria, and it joined Tristan de Luna's ships as they sailed from Mexico toward Pensacola." She hummed to herself as she read. Then she looked up. "It's the same information Owen told us. I don't see much else."

I spooned the batter onto the griddle and adjusted the temperature. "Did you find any societies or clubs for people who are into that stuff?" I peeked under the edges of the pancakes and flipped them when they browned.

Hazel tapped on the keys again. "I think so ... okay, here is one. The Society for Shipwrecks. Original name." She flashed a grin.

"Do they have a local chapter?"

More tapping. "Yes! One here in Pensacola. Guess what?" Her eyes twinkled.

"What?" I flipped the pancakes and slid them onto a plate before adding more batter to the griddle.

"They meet in an hour."

Not knowing what to wear to a club for shipwreck junkies, I went casual. Tan capris, black T, and I shoved a black ballcap on my head at the last minute.

Hazel used her phone's map app and plugged in the address for the meeting place.

"I think it's near the Bird Rescue Center." She used her fingertips to enlarge the map. "Wait a minute—it's at a marina right down the road from it."

Maybe Harry docked his boat there. I tried to figure out where he lived, but Pensacola had too many marinas. Besides, I had no clue what kind of boat he owned.

I pulled into the Blue Oyster Marina parking lot and found a spot near the entrance. This marina boasted live band nights, bingo championships, and more. According to the website, the Society for Shipwrecks met in room 2A. We didn't see anyone inside. Sparse lighting came from a few wall sconces.

"I thought they held a lot of meetings and events here. It's kind of strange that it's so dark." Hazel flipped on her phone's flashlight.

"How do we find the room?"

She wandered down the hall and read the number beside the first closed door. "This is 4D. Guess we keep walking."

I followed her, keeping my eyes and ears open. The quiet and emptiness of the place sent creepy crawlies skittering up my spine.

"Here it is." Hazel jiggled the doorknob. "It's locked." She turned to me. "Maybe the website information was old?"

Footsteps sounded, heading away from us.

"Hello! Anyone here?" I shouted.

My words echoed. No answer.

"We should leave," I said. The eerie atmosphere persisted, and more shivers ran through me.

"Let's look around some. They might be in a different room." Hazel led the way down another hall.

I looked over my shoulder, imagining someone had followed us.

After several minutes of searching, muted voices came, and we made our way toward them. Double glass doors leading to an outside deck were propped open. We walked through them and found three men and one woman seated at a patio table.

"Is this the shipwreck group?" Hazel asked.

Chapter 16

A man with thick, white hair, bright blue eyes, and a handlebar mustache rose from his seat. His cane tapped as he limped our way and held out a shaky hand. "Right here, young lady. I'm Ted Collins. What's your name?"

Hazel shook his hand and introduced us.

He, in turn, introduced his companions and pulled over two chairs for us to join them. They were a motley crew, not unlike our birding group.

"Whatcha doin' here tonight?" he asked. "We haven't had any new members in ..." He looked at the others and shrugged. "I can't remember when anyone new came."

"We saw the news about the shipwreck, and then we found your group." I wouldn't mention what we had unless I had to.

"Ah, yes," said a man who looked about my age. Stuart, if I remembered correctly. "The 'mysterious' caravel." He made air quotes, his lip curled in a sneer.

"What's mysterious about it?" Did Hazel practice that wide-eyed, innocent expression in the mirror?

The lone woman in the group, whom Ted introduced as

Ruth, chuckled. "So many things." She lifted her hand and counted off on her fingers. "First, why was it just discovered?"

I thought the tides had changed the bottom of the bay or that erosion had occurred. Since I knew little about any of this, I shrugged.

She cocked an eyebrow. "Second, have you heard any rumors about it?"

Hazel and I exchanged glances. I tipped my head at her. She was the expert in portraying innocence.

"Rumors?" She put her hand to her chest as if shocked by the question. "The news reported on the wreck but didn't mention rumors."

She wasn't lying.

Ted spoke up, his voice gravelly. "Rumors abound about the caravel."

Stuart leveled him with a glare. "We don't know if they're true." He huffed and sat back, arms crossed.

Ruth said, "Stop it, boys. Third, who is in charge of the recovery of the shipwreck?"

"Aren't there rules about recovering a wreck?" I asked.

The third man, Clay, smoothed his tie and spoke up. "Yes, but because the Caravel Santa Maria was a tagalong, and it wasn't registered like the rest of de Luna's group, those rules and rights are up in the air."

"How much?" I asked.

"What do you mean?" Ted propped his elbows on the table. "How much are the rights up in the air?"

"Yes." If there was a fight over who owned the caravel or who had the right to explore the wreck, and if it carried gold, that might be a motive for murder. If I could link all this together.

A lot of "ifs."

Stuart drummed his fingers on the table. "We're looking

into it."

No one else spoke.

Hazel glanced at me. "We are aware of some ... things."

"Like what?" Ruth narrowed her eyes.

"Well, like there might be a curse?" She gave an uninterested one-shouldered shrug.

Each of them gasped.

Stuart stood, his chair tipping over in his haste. "Do. Not. Ever. Mention. The. Curse."

I covered my mouth so he wouldn't see my smile. I felt the group's fear, and Stuart's serious tone and curtness told me these people weren't a hobby group. Did they have a stake in this caravel? My humor would not be appreciated. I coughed and said, "I'm sorry, we won't say that again."

He picked up his chair and sat.

"So," Hazel piped up, "why was it discovered?"

Ted and Clay offered their opinions. Storms, tides, erosion, and time were the causes, as I thought.

"And the rumors?" I hesitated to ask because, from what Maggie Turnball had said, people who possessed items from the shipwreck were cursed, and many died. I wouldn't mention the curse. Did I need to worry about the fact that we possessed coins from the wreck?

Certainly not.

I hoped not.

Stuart harrumphed, but Ruth said, "Apparently, gold and silver are on the ship."

Oh, that kind of rumor. I relaxed. They weren't talking about people dying.

"I think the news mentioned that too," Hazel said.

I knew before the news reported the discovery. We talked about it with Shortie. I didn't bring that up, either.

"How do you find out who owns the wreck?" I asked.

Clay stroked his beard. "In 1987, an act was passed called the Abandoned Shipwrecked Act. President Reagan signed it into law in 1988. Because of it, all shipwrecks in U.S. waters belong to the United States, not the people who discovered them."

"In Florida, the Bureau of Archaeological Research oversees these things," Ruth said.

"I heard that students and professors from the University here helped with the de Luna shipwrecks." Hazel frowned. "How did they do that?"

"They've been involved for maybe twenty years. The Florida BAR found the first de Luna ship, but students and professors from UWF helped recover it. Their archaeological students found the second and third ships," Ruth said.

"Are they helping with the caravel?" I asked.

Ted shook his head. "We're not sure. It's been in the news, so Florida Research and UWF personnel know about it. The wreck is visible, but no one is working on it yet." He held up his palms. "We talked about taking my boat and going out to see it. Y'all want to tag along?"

Hazel and I looked at each other. She wiggled her eyebrows, and I grinned.

"Sure," I said.

TED'S BOAT barely held the six of us. We squeezed into two groups of three, side-by-side. I trailed my fingers in the bayou as we motored into the bay. Gulls cried overhead as we passed fishing boats, sailboats, and Boston whalers.

Maybe these people would tell me if Harry docked his boat here. I didn't even have to lean over to ask Clay.

"Can you call a marina to find out if someone has a boat there?"

"Like at a hotel?" He rolled his shirtsleeves up. His beard waved in the breeze, and he tucked his tie inside the shirt's buttons.

"Yes, I guess."

He shrugged. "I think so? Hey Ted, can the marina tell you who docks there?" We sat so close, he didn't have to raise his voice.

"Pretty sure." Ted steered us along the coastline toward the wreck.

Up ahead, we saw part of the caravel above the waterline. That's what Cynthia and I saw from Fort Pickens. From what Hazel read and told me, the other de Luna ships, discovered by archaeologists and divers, were submerged.

We pulled alongside it, and Stuart cautioned us to keep our hands to ourselves, but we all pulled out our cell phones and took pictures. He leaned over and looked down through the water.

"I had a face mask, but Gabby took it." He sighed.

My ears perked up at the name. "Who is that?" I tried to sound nonchalant, but my heart raced. Gabby might be the one who tied them all together. Mentally, I rubbed my hands together with glee.

I remembered how she had run out when she heard about Kurt, and how she reacted, saying repeatedly, "It was an accident, it was an accident."

Ted waved his hand. "Gabby is Stuart's niece. She goes to UWF and majors in archaeology. Right, Stu? She's one of the ones who helped get us interested in shipwrecks. Sometimes, she and Stuart take my boat out to search for wrecks."

Stuart sat up. "Gabby is my favorite niece. She loves these

shipwrecks as much as I do." He leaned over again and cupped his hands around his face. "We got to see a little bit of the archaeological dig on the land that de Luna wanted to establish."

The boat tipped precariously, and we all let out a yelp.

"We need to head back. It's almost too dark to see." Ted started the motor.

Ruth leaned back in her seat. "Gabby was cousins with that boy, the one who died the other night over at the Bird Rescue Center."

A frosty trickle ran down my back. "I thought they were stepbrother and sister." I raised my voice and directed my words to Stuart.

"They were." His face turned red, his mouth twisted into a grimace.

Ruth leaned closer. "Gabby is related to those people on the news." She clicked her tongue. "Yeah, she tried to hide it, but she is Estelle Keaton's niece or granddaughter? I'm not sure. She worked at the rescue center because of them. They got her the job."

So, Gabby was Stuart's niece, and she was related to the Keatons? I needed a genealogy chart, because this didn't add up. Who else was related to Estelle and Roger Keaton?

"How do they know the ship had gold? The others didn't," Hazel said.

"Books about the de Luna group mentioned it," Stuart said.

Clay dropped his cell in his shirt pocket. "I think someone found some coins." He lowered his voice as if his words were meant for me alone.

I nudged Hazel, who nodded. She heard what he said, and then she shook her head. We still hadn't revealed that we possessed some coins. What books did Ruth refer to? Owen's hadn't mentioned any gold.

Ted turned the boat around and headed back to the

marina. The sun was setting, and I enjoyed the beautiful gold and orange streaks in the sky. A thought niggled at my brain. Cynthia and I saw the caravel when we went birding.

Cynthia. She never called or texted. My stomach flipped.

~

WE SAID goodbye to our new friends, and I hurried Hazel to my SUV. I called Cynthia over and over without any answer. My call didn't even go to voicemail.

"I bet her phone died." Hazel patted my arm.

I roared up the road. "She's been with Harry since I left over six hours ago." Had Harry dropped her at the house, and I worried for no reason?

"Will you try Carter?" I asked.

Hazel got his voicemail and left a brief message. "I'll text both of them."

We arrived at the Center, parked, and rushed to the building. No light shone through the windows, and we couldn't get inside.

"Any response on the texts?" I asked.

Hazel shook her head.

"Let's go around back." I prayed as we followed the path. Night had fallen, and the birds were quiet. "Surely she would tell me where she was."

As we passed the side of the building, Hazel pointed. "I'll try that door. Holler if you see anything."

No noise or movement out back. Even the frogs were quiet. I didn't see a boat. I walked back to Hazel, shoulders slumped, stomach roiling. Where was Cynthia?

Hazel stood in the side doorway. "I wanted to call for you. This door is open, and night lights are on. Let's go look."

The hallway brought us to the two rooms opposite each

other. I wiggled the doorknob to my left, but it remained locked. Cynthia and I had entered it the one time when we found the quetzal eggs. My hands trembled when I tried the storage room door. It opened easily and still held the cleaning supplies. I called Cynthia's name, keeping my voice low. Where could she be?

"Hazel, try her phone again." I rubbed my sweaty hands on my capris.

"No answer, Peg." Hazel's eyes shone with sympathy in the dim lighting.

I pinched my lips together. I wanted to scream my daughter's name, but the eerie silence stopped me. Shaking my shoulders and drawing a deep breath, I said, "Let's keep going."

Hazel held my hand as we made our way down the long hall. I tugged her toward the entrance, and we checked behind the lobby counter. We hurried through the exhibits but still couldn't find Cynthia.

"I guess we need to try Harry's office," Hazel said.

I nodded, following her to the door. She reached for the knob, and it turned. A whimper escaped me.

"I'm here with you." Hazel squeezed my shoulder.

I clenched my teeth and squeezed my hands until my nails bit into my palms. She pushed the door and flipped on the light. Harry's office was empty. I tipped my chin toward the inner room. "We have to check in there."

Hazel turned, her expression filled with fear.

"At least Kurt isn't inside." My lame joke fell flat.

"Let's do it together," she said.

We placed our hands on the knob and turned it. It didn't move.

"It's locked." I turned and slumped against the door.

Hazel beat her hands on the door and hollered, "Cynthia? Hello? Cynthia?" We stood and waited for any sound.

"We need to get inside that room." Visions of my daughter lying on the floor filled my mind. I looked around Harry's office. "What can we use to open that door?" A crowbar would be perfect. Or an axe. I turned to his desk and saw a key. I never imagined it would be so simple. I handed it to Hazel.

"Try this."

She inserted it into the lock. A breath whooshed out of both of us when it clicked, and the doorknob turned. She handed me the key, and we entered the room.

Chapter 17

Many times in my life, I imagined things would turn out one way, but everything went in a different direction. I vaguely remembered someone saying all this trouble started when I began the Empty Nesters Birding Group.

I didn't think that caused the problems.

Except here in Harry's inner office, I found my daughter's body.

Hazel gasped. Cynthia lay on her side, her hands tucked under her head as if she were asleep. I dropped to my knees beside her, dread curling through my body. "Cynthia, Cynthia!" Not my little girl! Please, God. I shook her shoulder and rolled her onto her back, checking for her pulse. "She's alive, Hazel! Call nine-one-one." I patted Cynthia's cheek, but she didn't respond.

I rocked back on my heels. How did this happen? My chest tightened, and nausea roiled in my stomach. "I should have made her come with me. I shouldn't have waited so long to check on her." My words ended in a wail.

Hazel called 911, joined me on the floor, and held one of Cynthia's hands. She rubbed her arm and muttered a prayer. I closed my eyes and sought peace through her words, but it wouldn't come. A black cloud swirled in my mind and blocked my feelings, my strength, my ability to pray.

I ground my teeth and drew in a deep breath. Exhaling hard, I said, "Where is Harry? He must be responsible for this." I jumped to my feet and hurried through the building again, calling his name. "When I get hold of you ..." I threatened. My hands shook, and I curled them into fists, my muscles quivering with frustration. He wasn't here. Or he wasn't answering.

At the same time I heard sirens, I remembered his missing boat. I rushed to the front door, unlocked it, and waved the EMTs inside.

"She's in here." I pointed.

The little room crowded quickly, and Hazel wormed her way out to where I stood. They assessed my daughter and lifted her onto a backboard. My gut clenched.

"Is she okay?" I swiped tears from my cheeks.

A female EMT stepped to my side. "Ma'am, this is your daughter?"

I nodded.

"My granddaughter," Hazel said.

"All right. Well, her pulse and blood pressure are slow. We'll take her to the hospital. Which do you prefer?"

"West Florida," Hazel and I said at the same time. The other EMTs carried the backboard into the lobby and transferred Cynthia onto a stretcher.

The EMT with us asked about any allergies. Then she said, "Drugs? Prior history?"

Another punch to the gut. "No!"

She lowered her head, eyebrows raised, lips pursed. But I knew my daughter.

Didn't I?

I shook my head. "Not that I know of. She just got out of the Navy. I left her here to help Dr. Harry. She was fine when I left ..." My words trailed off.

"Dr. Harry?"

"He works here," Hazel said. "She stayed behind to help him clean up."

"Gotcha. Okay, we'll take her to West Florida Hospital. You can meet us there." She joined her coworkers at their truck.

Hazel and I stepped into the parking lot, and I pulled the front door behind me. I stopped, ear cocked at a noise. "I think Harry is back. I hear the boat motor."

She followed me, her hand clutching my shirt. Total darkness enveloped us. I wanted to catch Harry before he escaped. My fingers itched to put them around his scrawny neck. Why did he hurt my daughter? What had he done to her?

I used the building's bricks as a guide. Without moonlight, nothing reflected off the water. I pulled to a stop and whispered, "Shh."

There. A tiny plop of water and a quiet grunt sounded as Harry climbed out of his johnboat. He approached, passing close enough to touch him. Hazel tapped my back, and we followed. He opened the side door, the inside light revealing his wet clothes.

"Where have you been? What did you do to Cynthia?" I lunged at him, desperate to have my questions answered.

Someone grabbed my arm and held me back.

"Let go of me, Haz— Oh, Marcus, thank God you're here. You need to arrest this man." I jabbed Harry in the chest.

Marcus stepped between me and my intended victim. I tried to look around him, but he blocked my view.

"Don't let him go!" I feared Harry would take off.

Harry stuck his head around one side of Marcus. "What are

you talking about, Peg? Where is Cynthia? Karla said she got a ride home."

Karla? What did she have to do with this?

I crossed my arms and stomped my foot. "Karla left before I did."

Hazel piped up, "Yes, she did."

Her words caught me off guard. She wasn't even with me then.

She leaned over and whispered, "I've got your back, Peg."

Marcus held out his arms. "How about we go in and figure out what's going on?" He gestured to Harry. "And you can put on some dry clothes."

Marcus stayed between me and Harry as we walked up the hall. Harry ducked into the men's room to dry off while we waited in the lobby. I leaned against the counter, arms crossed, glaring.

"I need to go to the hospital," I spit out. My daughter needed me. Now.

"You will," Marcus said. "Once I take your statement." His raised eyebrows stopped my protests.

Harry exited the bathroom and joined us. Hazel was the one person in the room not glaring at anyone.

Marcus took our statements. I held my tongue and didn't go after Harry again. I didn't believe him about Karla. He wasn't a trustworthy person. When Cynthia woke up, I would ask her and learn the truth.

"Can we go now?" I asked after Hazel and I told our side of the story.

"Yes. I'll be out to the hospital shortly to talk with Cynthia." Marcus leveled Harry with a stern look. "Do not leave Pensacola. I'll be back to talk to you."

～

CYNTHIA'S DOCTOR met with Hazel and me outside of her room. Young and handsome, he had an arrogant air about him. My knowledge of medical staff was limited to the few times I'd been in the hospital myself. He assured us she would be fine but that it would be several hours before she would be awake and lucid.

"What happened to her? Did you do bloodwork?" I still didn't believe she took drugs.

He crossed his arms. "Someone roofied her."

"Wait, what?"

"Rohypnol," he said.

"I know what being roofied means and the name of the drug." Okay, I didn't know the drug's name, but still, I was older than this guy. "How in the world did that happen?"

"Ma'am, I don't know."

Hazel's face paled. "Doctor," she said, her voice trembling, "was she raped?"

My heart pounded in my chest. "Why would you think that? She had her clothes on when we found her." Anger vied with sadness and mixed with fear. Did someone hurt Cynthia on top of drugging her? As if that wasn't bad enough.

"It's a valid question, but no, she wasn't."

Hazel and I let out heavy sighs.

"We checked because it is typically used as a date-rape drug. Or to knock someone out and make her unaware of her environment." The doctor turned to leave.

I grabbed his arm. "Hang on. How long will she be out?" I had more questions, and this guy seemed determined to leave them unanswered.

He stared at my hand until I let go. "A nurse will be in soon with more information." He walked away.

We sat with Cynthia and waited for her to come around. The nurse told us all about the drug and how Cynthia was lucky she hadn't been assaulted. I agreed, but why would someone drug my daughter?

THE HOSPITAL ADMITTED Cynthia for overnight observation. I sent Hazel home around three in the morning once Cynthia gave her limited side of the story. The drug affected short-term memory, so we weren't sure if she actually remembered what happened.

Dozing in the recliner wasn't very comfortable, but my thankfulness to be with my daughter outweighed the discomfort. I thought back over what had happened since we found out the Keatons were back in Pensacola.

Someone had threatened two of my kids. The anonymous caller had been in Chloe's hospital room and left a package at her house. This person knew me well enough to find her. Now, someone had knocked Cynthia out. Why were they after me and mine?

I'd gotten involved with the Keatons by accident last year. How was I to know that Estelle Keaton was jealous that one of our original birders—her old BFF—had claimed a hummingbird as her own find? It still amazed me that someone would kill over a tiny, quivering bird.

What Cynthia said when we drove to Fort Pickens ran through my mind. "How dangerous could birders be?" The memory lightened my heart. My little band of birders might not be dangerous, but some birders were—Estelle Keaton the most dangerous of all.

I woke up when a chirpy woman came in with Cynthia's breakfast tray.

"Hello, sunshine! How are we today?"

I rubbed my eyes. *We* are tired. "Today is a new day. How

are you?"

"Blessed! I'm blessed. Thank you for asking." She set the tray on Cynthia's table, uncovered the food, and wiped her hands in a manner that reminded me of Mary Poppins. "I'll see you later, darlings!" She waved and left our room.

Cynthia and I stared at each other before bursting out laughing.

"She's a bright spot in the day," I said.

Cynthia pushed up in the bed and shifted her legs over its edge. "Yes, she is. I need to go to the bathroom. Can you help me? I still feel shaky."

Bitter emotions rushed in and smothered the morning's bright beginning. I smushed them down. "Sure, honey."

Together, we got her in the bathroom, and she managed to stand afterward and wash her hands and face. She came out, brushing her hair back. "I feel like a new woman," she said.

I hugged her tight. "I am so glad you're okay."

She and I sat on the edge of her bed and shared her breakfast. After that, we waited. And waited. Hazel called. Shortie called. Carter and Chloe checked in. The nurse kept saying they were getting the paperwork together, but it took forever. We lay on the bed, side by side, and dozed.

Lunchtime came and went before the nurse arrived with Cynthia's discharge paperwork and a list of dos and don'ts.

"If anything feels off, you need to come back." The nurse handed the folder to me. "Keep an eye on her, Mom."

That wouldn't be a problem. I'd watch my daughter like a hawk. I texted Hazel to come for us. When she arrived, I crawled into the backseat of her VW so Cynthia didn't have to climb in there.

"You may have to pry me out of here." I popped my head between the two front seats.

She turned. "Not quite as flexible as me, huh?"

I burst out sobbing.

"Mom, Mom, I was kidding!" She shifted in her seat and tried to hug my head.

"It's okay. I'm okay. Ouch, you're squishing me."

She giggled and let go. "Why are you crying?"

I mopped tears off my face with a towel from the back seat. When I dropped the towel, dog fur stuck to my face. I wiped it and the rest of the tears off with my hands. "It's just so much. Last night, I thought about how the Keatons have done so many bad things."

"Especially Estelle," Hazel said.

"Yes, exactly. She was the one behind Sylvia's death and Anna's too, even though that wasn't intended. All over a little bird. Now she's after me and you guys." Tears flowed again.

Hazel pulled into the garage as I spoke. She turned off the Bug, and she and Cynthia both turned to me.

"It's the quetzal," they said together.

Chapter 18

The doctor ordered Cynthia to rest for the next two days. The drug would work its way out of her system, but she needed to be mindful of any aftereffects. I watched her closely until she told me to leave her alone.

She didn't remember who gave her the drug. She shook her head when I asked if she had seen Karla or Harry. Amnesia, a common side effect of Rohypnol, limited her memories, and I didn't want to badger her into saying someone was there when she wasn't sure.

When we arrived home, Hazel got her laptop from her room while I headed to the shower. I was tired but wanted to learn more about quetzals and their link to the Keatons. I dressed and found her at the table, laptop open, notebook and pen beside her.

"We need to make lists. They helped us last time." She pushed a seat out for me.

I hoped she was right. Estelle Keaton had messed with my family for the last time. My mamma bear was wide awake and ready.

Hazel found her notes that she'd written about the quetzal

mystery a few weeks ago. "Last fall, one quetzal went missing from a Guatemalan zoo. The day of Chloe's shower, we learned the Keatons were back in Pensacola."

"Don't forget about the caravel and the coins." I pointed to her notebook. "Add that. I think those coins are part of this. If we can find how the quetzals, Estelle, and the coins connect, we should be able to solve this mystery."

"You believe in the curse?" she asked as she added the information.

"No, of course not." I frowned. "Do you?"

"No ..." She made a face. "It's weird, though, isn't it? Roger died, Kurt died, someone threatened your girls ..." She sighed. "Nope, I don't believe in curses."

I giggled at her words. After all she said, it would be easy to think the rumors about the coins were true, but I didn't think so.

Hazel ran her finger over the list. "Next, Cynthia found the feather, and I found Roger." She shivered and rubbed her arms. "Ugh, that was horrible."

I leaned over and hugged her. No one enjoyed finding dead bodies.

"The last thing I wrote was Dr. Harry acted so strange about the feather."

Thinking about the man made me mad all over again. "Is he innocent in all of this?"

"He's very odd." She shifted in her chair and stared out the window.

"Mhmm. Very." I tapped her pen on the notebook. "Let's organize the list." I wrote "Suspects" on the left side of the page, "Motive" in the middle, and "Opportunity" on the right side. Under the first category, I jotted down three names—Dr. Harry, Estelle Keaton, and Gabby.

"I forgot about Gabby," Hazel said. "Who else should we add?"

"I can't think of anyone else. But we weren't aware of the mayor until the last minute, last time. With Estelle, anyone could be part of this."

A knock at the door startled me. I frowned and rose to open it. Marcus stood on my doorstep, fist raised for another round of knocking.

"Don't you check the peephole?" He glared.

Oops. Mental reminder to do that. "Usually?"

His eye twitched. "Can I come in?"

I stepped back and waved him inside. "You can join us at the table. Hazel and I are working on a list of suspects, motives, and opportunities."

In the past, Marcus would have warned us to let the police department do the work, but today, he nodded. "Good idea."

"What in the world?" Hazel whispered.

Marcus cleared his throat. "I'm here on official business. Is Cynthia up to talking more about what happened?"

He was sparing her from a trip to the police department. I was glad to have him as a friend—well, not a friend, but someone who cared about me and my family. I thanked him and went to wake my daughter.

WHILE CYNTHIA TALKED WITH MARCUS, I prepared spaghetti, salad, and garlic bread and was dishing it out when Carter came home. Marcus left with his ever-present notepad, and the four of us sat to eat. Hazel held out both hands, indicating we should all join hands.

"We need to pray and thank God," her voice trembled, "that our Cynthia wasn't hurt worse and that we are all together." She prayed, and her heartfelt words made us all sniffle.

I passed the bread. "What have you been up to today?" I asked Carter.

"Helping Shortie after he got off work."

"You did?" It occurred to me that I hadn't talked to Shortie since everything happened with the shipwreck society and Cynthia.

Carter bit off a huge bite of garlic toast. "Yeah," he mumbled around his food, "he said he would call you tonight." He tipped his head to Hazel's laptop and notebook, which she had shoved to the side of the table. "What are you up to, Grandma?"

We filled him in on our short list of suspects. His eyes grew round, and he choked on his spaghetti. He gulped his water. "You guys have gotten in way over your heads."

He'd been hanging around Shortie all right. I held up my hand. "Now wait a minute." I showed him our notes and explained the connections.

"Your suspects are Dr. Harry, Estelle Keaton, and Gabby? Who is Gabby?"

"Kurt's stepsister." Cynthia grimaced.

"She's Stuart's niece," Hazel offered.

Cynthia and Carter both piped up, "Who is Stuart?"

I explained about the Society for Shipwrecks members who met at the Blue Oyster Marina.

"Just what you need is another group of weir—interesting people." Cynthia winked. She stood and gathered plates.

"They were interesting. I don't know how the relationship goes, but one of them mentioned that Gabby got her job at the Center through ..." I snapped my fingers. "I remember now. Gabby is Estelle Keaton's niece, and she helped her get the job at the Center."

Hazel turned to me. "Niece? But she's Stuart's niece."

"Oh, I think I have the family relationships mixed up."

Cynthia stacked the dishes in the sink. "Remember what Gabby said when you found Kurt? She kept saying it was all an accident." She returned to the table, sat, and pulled the notebook toward her. "We are missing something here."

Hazel giggled and slapped her hand over her mouth when Cynthia glared at her. "You remind me so much of your mother, dear." Her lips twitched.

"I find that to be a compliment. Carter, do the dishes. We have some murders to figure out."

Carter saluted her without a word. Years ago, he learned to go with the flow with his bossy sisters.

Cynthia picked up the pen and notebook and flipped to a clean sheet of paper. "Let's figure out this relationship between Stuart, Gabby, and Estelle." She wrote "Stuart" with a line below his name to Gabby. Then she wrote Estelle's name near his with another line to Gabby.

"So, how are Stuart and Estelle related?" Hazel asked.

"And where does Kurt come in?" I asked.

"Do you have Stuart's number?" Cynthia tapped the pen on his name.

I shook my head. "No, and he didn't seem to like me."

Carter spread the kitchen towel out to dry and joined us at the table. "Everyone likes you, Mom."

"True." I grinned. I checked my phone. "It's Monday today. I can't believe we met the Shipwreck people yesterday. I had an appointment today, I think." I couldn't remember what it was, but the nagging sensation wouldn't leave. I checked the calendar on my phone.

"Oh, no." I groaned, a hard knot forming in my stomach.

"What?" Hazel asked. "What's wrong?"

None of my family knew about Lauree's diagnosis, but I just remembered we'd scheduled a lunch date for today.

"Lauree and I were supposed to have lunch this afternoon." My voice shook, and I bit my tongue to keep the tears at bay. My best friend and I had failed her.

"She won't mind, Mom." Cynthia waved her hand like my slipup wasn't important. "She understands how you are."

"What does that mean?"

"Well, she knows you. How you are." Cynthia backpedaled.

Carter jumped in to help. "It's just that you are … you."

"Hmm." I stood and peeked out the blinds. The sun hadn't set yet. "I'm going over to her house and apologize." CB followed me outside and trailed behind me as I walked to Lauree's.

She sat on their hanging glider on the front porch. She patted the seat beside her, and I joined her, CB lying at our feet. The gentle swinging, the soft June breeze, and the setting sun calmed my spirit. Lauree would understand that I hadn't meant to blow her off. I opened my mouth to apologize, and she raised her hand.

"First, I forgive you for forgetting our lunch date. I know how you are. Something important came up, I'm sure." She turned toward me, her amber eyes reflecting the last bit of sun. "I love you, Peg, but I need *you* now. You." She reached over and gripped my hand, holding on tightly.

Tears filled my eyes. I bowed my head and said a prayer for strength. I sniffled, squeezed her hand, and met her eyes. "I'm here. Right now and always. What do you want to talk about?" I had to put my issues aside and be there for my friend.

We spent the next half hour talking about some of the most heart-rending things I ever imagined discussing.

"John can handle the kids if I die," she said. "I want you to be their aunt, not their second mom." She stopped and examined our clasped hands. "John might remarry. He says he won't, but he might. I would want him to as long as she loved our kids like they were hers."

I understood the other side of this—being the one left behind. I remembered what I'd been through trying to raise my children without Zack. Lauree had been by my side then. I never even considered dating until mine were grown and gone.

"I'll vet them all," I promised. How would I do this without her? My heart cracked a little more.

She giggled. "I expect you to. You better do a good job of it." She listed several requirements for a prospective new wife and mom for her kids.

"Lauree?" I didn't want to ask, but we'd been talking for a while now, and she still hadn't told me details from this afternoon's appointment. "What did you find out today?"

Her face paled, and she shook her head. "I haven't told John. I don't know how to."

My heart sank. My legs felt like lead, and acid roiled through my stomach. *Not Lauree, God. Please.* I took a deep breath, stood, and held out my hand, prepared to do the hard stuff. "Let's go inside and talk to him. I'm with you."

Chapter 19

I'd been through plenty in my life, starting with Zack's death when our kids were so young. I thought that was the hardest thing, but watching John's cheerful face change with Lauree's words was the worst thing I had ever experienced.

While they held each other and mourned a future that had changed with a test and doctor's appointment, I left, closing the door tight behind me. I went to my front porch, sank into the rocker, buried my head in my hands, and wept.

Miracles happen, and I believe that. But my heart told me the truth. I didn't like it.

"Are you sure, God? Lauree? She's the best." God didn't "take" people based on their goodness—or badness. He didn't look at the Earth and do eeny, meeny, miny, moe. God was good. He loved Lauree, and He loved me. His ways were kind and just and good. And I knew His ways were high above mine, as were His thoughts.

I learned a verse at Vacation Bible School as a little girl. I recited it now, *"For my thoughts are not your thoughts, neither are your ways my ways, declares the Lord. As the heavens are higher than the earth, so are my ways higher than your ways and my thoughts than your thoughts."*

Gentle peace covered me. I prayed for my friend and her family with a fervency I never had before. Time was short. I accepted that or tried to. In the meantime, I would pray and love my dearest friend.

The front door opened, and CB bounded out, followed by Hazel. He ran to the lawn to do his business.

"You gonna scoop that up now or tomorrow?" I asked.

She jumped and clenched her fists. "Why are you out here?" She reached inside, flicked on the front porchlight, leaned over, and searched my face. "Why are you sitting in the dark? What's the matter, Peg?"

I shook my head. "It's Lauree. It's bad."

Hazel sunk to the front step and listened as I told her what I'd learned. CB joined us, stretching out at my feet. Hazel patted his silky ears while she took in my words. She kept repeating, "I can't believe it. Not Lauree."

I agreed wholeheartedly.

I finished and asked, "What time is it?"

"Almost midnight when I came outside. The kids are asleep."

My kids. I'd have to tell them. My shoulders slumped as another weight hit me. They loved Lauree, and all three called her "Mom." How would they handle this?

"Oh, Hazel, what do I do?" More tears fell.

She reached up and took my hand. "We pray, dear. That's what we do."

Exhaustion overwhelmed me, but my brain ran at high speed. I did deep breathing exercises. The last thing I remembered was studying the picture above my dresser—an old map of the Gulf Coast. Strange ideas of quetzals, caravels, and bird eggs mixed with memories of Lauree, and I slept.

I jerked awake when someone called my name. Sun shone through my bedroom windows, but no one was in my room.

"Peg!" It came again. The voice sounded odd, and I did not recognize it.

I sat up and pushed off my covers, trying to figure out where the voice came from.

"Peg, are you here?"

I thought the voice came from the back deck right outside my bedroom. I unlatched the window and pushed it up. "Who's out here? Lauree, is that you?" I looked side to side but couldn't see every part of the yard or deck.

Someone groaned, "I need help."

I flinched at the pain in the voice. Was it Lauree? It didn't sound like her, but my heart raced. No time to put on a robe over my PJs. I ran out of my room, tore open the back sliding door, and skidded to a stop on the empty deck.

"Hello? Lauree, is that you?" I hurried down the steps and checked the yard. "Hello?" I called again. No answer, and my backyard was empty. A rustling noise came from my left, and CB raced around the right corner of the house. Hazel followed close behind, calling his name. He rushed by me and headed for the marsh. Hazel stopped and crossed her arms.

"That dog. He heard noises and took off."

"Someone called my name. They said they needed help. I don't know who it was."

Hazel's eyebrows rose. "Did you recognize the voice?"

"No." A sob broke through. I pointed to Lauree's house. "I thought it was her. That she had been hurt." I leaned over, hands on my knees, and tried to catch my breath. It wasn't

Lauree, I repeated in my head. She's okay. I mentally stomped on the words "for now."

While bent over, I noticed something caught on an old chair under the deck. I squatted and picked it up.

"What's that?" Hazel shaded her eyes.

I stood and showed her. "I didn't see this until now. I wonder if whoever was out here dropped it."

"You really think someone tricked you?"

I grimaced and shrugged one shoulder. "I was awake the last three times they called me. Maybe they hid under the deck." I explained the noise that came from the left of the house before she and CB came from the right. I fingered the delicate gold chain and the sapphire and diamond pendant. "I think this is real jewelry."

Hazel clomped up the deck stairs and clicked her tongue for CB. I joined her and held out the necklace. The jewels sparkled in the early morning sunlight. And something else glittered. I handed the jewelry to Hazel.

"Do you see what's entwined in that chain?"

She held it out, and her eyebrows shot up. "You don't think ...?"

I nodded. "I do. We need to call Marcus."

"What are you doing, Mom? You left the door open." Cynthia slid it shut behind her. "We'll have bugs and critters in the house."

"Someone called me." I shook my head. "And then we found this." I held up the necklace.

"I've been up for a couple of hours. I didn't hear anyone." Cynthia stepped closer and squinted. "I've seen that." She tapped her lip with one finger.

I pointed to the yard below my bedroom window. "Someone kept saying my name—out here. I came out, afraid Lauree had called me for help."

Hazel nodded. "CB heard noises too. That's why he took off." She called him again, and he emerged from the bushes behind my house. He trotted up the deck stairs, panting.

Cynthia's brows furrowed. "Wait, why would Lauree call for help?"

I sighed. I was about to break her heart, and she had no idea.

"Let's go inside." I didn't want any of my friend's family to hear what I said. I didn't know when they'd tell the twins, and I didn't want it to come from overhearing me. "I have some news," I began. She started crying before I said much. I'm sure my expression conveyed how bad things were. By the time I finished with the news, Carter had joined us.

"Mom, that can't be true." Carter swiped tears off his cheeks. "Not Ms. Lauree." His words ended in a moan.

I hugged him to me. "I'm so sorry."

"How long have you known?" Cynthia asked.

"She told me a couple of weeks ago that she had breast cancer. Yesterday, she found out she only has a couple of months. She didn't want me to tell anyone until now." I held my palms up. "I'm sorry, but I needed to honor that."

Her eyes glimmered with sadness. "What do we do?"

Hazel raised her hand. "The best thing we can do is pray. Why don't we set up a meal train? Or at least plan it."

"Carter and I can do that," Cynthia said. They went to her room to figure out how to set up one online.

Hazel tipped her head toward the table. "We need to call Marcus about this necklace."

"And figure out if it belongs to who we think it does."

Hazel fingered the hair stuck in the chain. "Sure looks like neon green to me."

~

I LEFT a message for Marcus and headed for my room, hoping a quick shower, brushing my teeth, and changing into clean clothes would help me face the day.

When I came out, Hazel had coffee ready. She handed me a mug and gestured toward the oven. "I made a simple breakfast casserole."

"Yum." I sipped my coffee, and my stomach growled. "Dinner last night was a long time ago. I don't even remember what we had."

"Spaghetti. You liked it."

I took a seat at the bar. "Where's your notebook?" A distraction from Lauree's painful news might help.

She grabbed it off the dining table and sat beside me. She turned to the page where we were attempting to figure out Stuart, Gabby, and Estelle's relationships.

"Estelle is in her early sixties. Stuart looked to be in his forties?" she asked.

"I think so. Several years younger than me."

She drew a line from him to Estelle. "She could be his aunt." She wrote Kurt's name and drew a line between him and Gabby.

"We need to contact someone for Stuart's phone number," I said. "Did the website you found for the Society of Shipwrecks give any local contact information?"

Hazel searched for that, and I rescued the breakfast casserole and called the kids to eat. I dished out four plates and made a fresh pot of coffee. One pot wouldn't be enough for the day.

Carter and Cynthia grabbed their plates and retreated into her room. CB limped after them.

I pointed it out to Hazel. She called him to her side and ran her hands down his leg. "It's not hot, and he doesn't whimper or pull away from me." She sat back on her barstool. "He probably stepped on a rock or in a hole in the marsh."

"I wish he could tell me what he spotted out there." I looked at CB. "Bark once if you saw a bad guy."

He barked.

Hazel and I laughed. "You're a nut," I told him, giving him a good ear rub.

While we ate, Hazel called the Society for Shipwreck's local number. Ted answered and passed Stuart's number on. He asked why we needed it, but Hazel kept her answer vague. She hung up and looked at me.

"Do we call him now?"

I shrugged. "Might as well. Let's see if we can connect these people."

My phone dinged with an incoming text from Marcus requesting my presence at the police station. How could my morning be more complicated? I slipped on my red sandals, filled a travel mug with coffee, and jotted Hazel a note. She was on the phone with Stuart, who, from what I overheard, was expounding on shipwrecks and coins. She rolled her eyes at me when I showed her my message.

On the way to the police station, I flipped through the reasons Marcus wanted to talk to me. I came up with outrageous ones—he was arresting me for drugging Cynthia, to even more bizarre—he was arresting me for killing Roger Keaton.

Or, possibly, he had found and arrested Estelle Keaton.

I sat up straight at the thought. How could I have forgotten about her? In all the craziness and grief of the last few days, Estelle hadn't crossed my mind except for her relationship with Stuart and Gabby.

She had some audacity returning to Pensacola, knowing

she was the prime suspect in two murder investigations. She and her husband might even be involved with the caravel and coins. And the quetzal. If all of that was true, who killed Roger? And where was the bird?

And was that neon green hair in the necklace Gabby's?

I had so many questions and no answers.

Chapter 20

I parked in the police station parking lot and fished the baggie out of my purse. Sunshine filtered through the windshield, caught the jewels, and set them sparkling. The pieces of green hair were still twined around the chain. I snapped a picture of it before walking inside the building. My plan—wait to hear what Marcus said. Then, I would show him the baggie and its contents.

My brain took a vacation when I sat in an interrogation room with him. And it wasn't his dimple flashing that caused it.

"Is that window one of those people can see through?" I waved. "They know I know they're there, right?" I offered my biggest smile, sitting like someone was taking my picture.

Marcus pulled a chair out and sat, arms crossed over his broad chest.

I held out the baggie to him. "Look what I found this morning." My brain screamed, "Take it back, take it back! This was not the plan!"

His eyebrow cocked, he reached out and took it. "What is it?"

"A necklace. Marcus ..."

"Detective Sharp."

I giggled. "Right, so those people—" I thumbed toward the window. "Don't realize we're friends." I sat back and shot him an exaggerated wink.

He laid down the baggie and leaned across the table, palms flat, eyebrows lowered. "Peg ... er, Ms. Howard, I mean Mrs." He sighed and thunked his head on the table.

"Yes, Mrs. Howard, thank you." This had been a bone of contention since we first met.

"Peg—" He looked up and whispered, "Please work with me here."

I snatched back the baggie, shoved it into my purse, and folded my hands on the table. "Detective Sharp, may I ask why you called me in today?"

He sat up, back straight. "Thank you," he mouthed. Aloud, he said, "Yes, ma'am, Mrs. Howard. I wanted more information from you on Estelle Keaton." He cocked his head and pulled his notepad and pen from his breast pocket.

Hmm. Estelle. I was right. What else could I tell him, though?

"What do you want to know? She was behind Anna and Sylvia's deaths. I think she might have killed her husband."

He rubbed his chin. "Why do you think that?"

"Because of her track record."

"What else?"

I wracked my brain. Did he know what happened with Dr. Harry, the quetzal eggs, and Estelle's relationship to Gabby? I asked him, and he shook his head.

"No, tell me about that. Start with Gabby. We're still looking for her." He looked up from his notes. "Please forget I said that." He looked at the window and sighed.

If they hadn't found Gabby, she might have been in my

backyard this morning. I tucked that information in the back of my mind and explained how Cynthia and I had found the quetzal eggs at the Center. I told him how quetzals were near threatened and how that meant they might become endangered in the near future. I rambled, but his expression never changed.

I told him about the birds, what we'd seen, how weird Dr. Harry acted, and on and on. I took out the baggie and handed it back to him, telling him what I thought about the chance Gabby had been in my backyard that morning. I thought he would be interested.

I was being gabby. I finally wound down.

"Is there anything else you need to know?" I asked. *Come on, Marcus, I've told you everything. Why are you staring at me like that?*

He shook his head, stood, and approached my side of the table. "Will you stand up please?"

I did.

He twirled his finger, indicating I needed to turn my back to him.

I did what he wanted.

He took hold of my hands and leaned close to my ear.

"Don't look around, and don't ask questions. You aren't safe. When you leave here, go to a hotel. I'll bring you some things. Don't argue with me." He frog-marched me to the door. "Ditch your cell phone so no one can track you. Kurt Lynch is part of the problem. I'll tell you more later."

I hurried to my car. All I could think was that I had never heard Kurt's last name before.

As I drove by the Escambia County jail that sat beside the police station, I noticed it did not look like any I'd seen on television. The place was big. I shuddered, imagining what it would be like to be arrested and have to stay inside.

Marcus didn't give me any idea where to go. He was probably as surprised as I was that I'd followed his advice. I drove around the block, found a dumpster, and tossed in my cell phone. The area I was in offered little in the way of places to stay. Most of the nicer hotels were closer to the beach area. Several streets away from the jail, I found a small motel, paid for a room, and called him from the outdated rotary dial phone in my room.

"Marcus, I can't stay here." I attempted to reason with him.

"I'm trying to keep you safe." His words came out in a growl. "Wait for me. I'll be there soon."

"This place—" I glanced at the shabby carpet and worn bedspread— "is something else. Are you sure I need to be here?" Who else could I call for help? "I want to call Shortie."

"I already told him what's happening," he said.

"You did?" Something smelled fishy. Marcus was withholding information.

"I did. I'll stop by soon, okay? Shortie is on his way. I'll text him where you are. Trust me."

"I don't trust you." I spit out the words, then stopped short. He wanted to keep me safe. Maybe I should pay attention to what he said.

"Please, Peg. I'll straighten this out." He cleared his throat.

"Straighten *what* out? That's what I don't understand, Marcus. None of this makes any sense."

He huffed. "Someone placed an anonymous phone call to the mayor."

I strained to hear him. "Anonymous caller?" I plopped onto the bed. Now I knew something was wrong.

"Um-hmm."

Marcus refused to tell me more about the caller and the mayor's involvement. I begged and pleaded, but he wouldn't budge.

Well then. The anonymous caller had once more ruined my day.

STAYING in a sketchy motel gave me plenty of time to think. And since that's all I could do, I reviewed last year's murders, which Estelle masterminded. The mayor we had then had committed them. Now he was in jail. Or prison. I'd have to ask to be sure. I wouldn't ask Marcus, though.

From all accounts, the mayor's replacement had passed strict background checks and wasn't mentally unbalanced like his predecessor. But apparently, someone had put a bug in his ear. Possibly about me killing Roger and Kurt.

That person held some kind of power over this new mayor, and I needed to find out what it was. How would I do that tucked away in this seedy place? I had no resources at this point.

I dozed on the bed and was startled awake by a knock on the door. "Who is it?"

"Me, Peg. Open up."

I jerked open the door to find Marcus on the doorstep.

"You couldn't find anything besides this flea trap?" he asked.

"You told me to go stay somewhere. You didn't tell me where. And this part of town isn't exactly known for its family-friendly vacation places."

He stuck out his hand.

"What?" I asked.

"Keys." He sighed. "You absolutely have to stay here. I'll park your car at the station. You dumped your phone?"

"Yes." Literally. I found my keys and held them above his hand. "You're sure about this?"

"I am. One of my people will be out here to guard you. You won't see him."

Oh, boy. My life had turned into a television show. A bad one. A small diner was attached to the motel. I looked both ways when I walked to it. Marcus said I wouldn't see my guard, and he was right. No one was in sight.

Dinner choices were limited, but I went with meatloaf, green beans, mashed potatoes, and a small bowl of peaches. I carried the food back to my room and pretended Cynthia had cooked it.

With my stomach full, I napped, although the bed wouldn't receive a high rating. Hard as wood, a thin mattress separated me from the frame and bunkie board. A kindergarten naptime mat came to mind. Comfort wasn't a high priority in the place.

A quiet tapping noise woke me. I jumped up, pulled the curtain aside, and found Shortie outside. I unlocked the door, and he rushed in and held me.

"I didn't kill anyone," I said, my face smashed against his shoulder. Tears burned my eyes and trickled down my cheeks. "Marcus says I should trust him. That he's trying to keep me safe."

"I know." He rubbed my back and didn't let go.

I hoped he never would. Once I brushed my teeth, I'd give him a big kiss. Backing out of his hold, I talked without breathing in his direction.

"Did you bring me anything? A toothbrush, hairbrush?"

His lips tipped up, and he shook a small makeup bag. "Hazel packed this for you."

I set it on my bed and shouted, "Yay!" when I saw what he brought. I laid out each item with careful precision. "Toothbrush, toothpaste, a hairbrush, wet wipes, and oh, my." I tucked the underwear under my top, heat rising up my neck and flooding my face.

Shortie shuffled his feet.

I shoved the toothbrush in my mouth. "Fank you." I rinsed and spit before joining him in the 'living room' and planting a kiss on his lips. "Thank you for bringing all this. How is Hazel? How are my kids?"

We perched side by side on the bed.

"It's been three days since I've seen you, but it feels like forever." He brushed my hair back. "I'm sorry I've been so busy. This car stuff has taken more time than I thought it would."

I leaned against his shoulder. "It's okay. You're here now. Please tell me what's happening at home." I needed him to distract me.

"Hazel told the kids you're safe, Chloe too. She said she didn't want to tell Lauree yet. She wouldn't tell me why." His words ended in a questioning tone.

I didn't want to tell him about Lauree's diagnosis right now. I waved my hand. "I'll call her when I can."

He shifted on the bed. "Did you know Marcus would want you to hide away?" His eyes searched mine.

"Not at all. He asked me to come to the station. Under false pretenses." I was still sour about Marcus.

"Did he say why?"

I dropped my head. "No, and I didn't ask. I assumed he wanted to talk about the case and Estelle. I never dreamed he would make me come here."

"He said someone called the mayor anonymously. How would that sway the police?" Shortie clicked his tongue. "Has to be Estelle behind this, right? This is her MO."

Modus Operandi. He was right about Estelle using people. I shrugged and stood. "I agree, but I don't understand any of this. And I don't know how involved the police are. Just Marcus. He's the only one I talked to." I gestured to the tiny room. "I found this place myself."

"Yeah." He patted his legs and stood. "I'll do whatever I can to help you."

I knew he would. We may not have said those three little words, but I thought we both felt them.

"You believe I'm innocent, right? I don't know anything else about either murder."

He took both of my hands and held them between us. "Peg, I've always believed in you."

My heart melted. He hugged me hard. His gentle kiss left me wanting more.

In a romantic movie, when two star-crossed lovers leave each other, they hold hands as long as possible, and then just their fingertips touch. We did that. It wasn't romantic at all. Desperation was a better description.

The motel room door clicked shut behind him, and I was alone. Again. I looked up. "You got this, right? You know I'm innocent. Please make a way for everyone else to believe it and for me to be safe." I brushed tears from my cheeks, sat on the hard bed, and huddled under a thin blanket. Hours later, I slept.

Chapter 21

No sunshine or chirping birds started my day, only a gray and gloomy sky. Coffee would wake me up, I hoped. I traipsed down to the diner, still no guard in sight, and grabbed a cup to go. "Good morning," the cashier said.

"Good morning to you." I stretched. Every muscle, joint, and tendon popped and snapped and complained. I needed to grab some ibuprofen. "I'll be right back."

After finding a bottle of pain relievers, I picked up a sausage biscuit too. I paid and returned to my room. "This looks yummy." I usually talked to Hazel, CB, or Roscoe when I ate. Today, I'd have to be my own company.

The biscuit wasn't half bad. The meal would get more stars than the bed. When I finished, I stuffed the wrapper in the tiny, dented trashcan.

After I ate, I showered and brushed my teeth and hair, thankful for the toothbrush and especially for the clean underwear Hazel had sent. I peeked through the curtains and watched rain puddle in the pitted parking lot. I had never been so alone in my life. Alone and desperate for answers.

Even when Carter first left for college, I had options. I

started the Empty Nesters Birding Group and filled my life with new friends.

Now, I had zero choices.

Who killed Roger? And Kurt. I wished I had Hazel's notebook and a pen. I liked to write or type my thoughts out. A glance around the room showed no writing tools, not even the typical notepad and pen most hotels offered. I considered my toothbrush. In movies, jailbirds sharpened the end of the toothbrush and used it as a shank. I wanted to write, not kill anyone.

I wouldn't mind kicking Marcus, but even though I was angry at him, I didn't want to kill him. He could take a turn in this rundown, old motel, though.

I sighed. Mentally, I opened a notebook and started thinking my notes.

I went back to who killed Roger and where Estelle might be. I imagined she had hidden out, laid low. Thinking about the family tree we wrote between Gabby, Stuart, and Estelle, going by ages, Estelle might be Stuart's grandmother or great-aunt. I already knew Gabby was his niece.

Was Estelle using Gabby as her hitman this time? Apparently, Estelle had no qualms about who she hurt.

What if Gabby shot Roger, stuck him on the blue tarp, and somehow got him over to Fort Pickens? She would need help and a boat.

Kurt's face flashed through my mind. He might have helped. And Stuart had access to Ted's boat.

"Then she got rid of Kurt because he knew too much," I whispered. If Stuart also helped, would she go after him? Maybe, unless he was in cahoots with her.

I closed the notebook in my mind, lay down, and put my arm over my eyes. Marcus—Detective Sharp—had been vague about the anonymous caller. He implied that someone had said I had been involved in Roger and Kurt's murders. But I didn't think he believed that. And I hadn't been arrested.

I sat up. What about alibis? They would have ruled me out as a suspect. When had Roger been killed? I reopened my mental notebook and wrote:

First, did the coroner or ME have a time of death for Roger? If I found that out, I could figure out where I was at the time.

Second, were the police informed that I didn't own a gun? Roger was shot, and they would know what weapon was used and try to match it. I put a little checkmark on the thought because I would pass that test.

Third, Kurt's last name was Lynch. Someone else I met had the same last name, but who?

Fourth, I discovered Kurt's body. Did Marcus think I faked my reaction? Did the police ever find Gabby, who kept saying, 'It was an accident!'? Marcus said they hadn't and acted like he shouldn't have told me. Unless he was setting me up to see my reaction.

Fifth, I returned to the family tree between great-aunt Estelle, nephew Stuart, and great-niece Gabby, Kurt's stepsister. What a convoluted tree. I shook my head. Dr. Harry —did he fit in it anywhere? Or was he just an odd duck?

Another person hovered in the back of my mind. One other name I couldn't access—someone who gave me the creeps and acted strangely.

A knock sounded on my door. "Just want you to know I'm still here," a man said.

"Oh?"

"Your boyfriend came to visit you."

"Yes, Marcus told him where I was."

"Huh." Footsteps sounded, heading away from my door.

I tiptoed to the window and pulled back the curtain. "Why

would his guard come talk to me?" He'd stayed invisible before. Should I call Marcus and ask?

THE FOLLOWING day began the same way—sausage biscuit and coffee. I hadn't had any other visitors the day before except the guard who talked to me through the door. I polished off the food. It may not be five-star, but I had nothing else to do besides eat. The night before, I thought about exercising to pass the time. I tried one pushup and came close to breaking my nose on the dirty carpet when my non-muscly arms failed me. Jumping jacks sounded like more effort than I wanted to expend. I ended up dozing for most of the day.

Today was a new day. I pretended Hazel sat beside me and discussed what I had scheduled for the day.

"I'm going to ask the first person who comes to see me for some paper and a pencil."

Pretend Hazel nodded and gave me a thumbs up.

"I'll write down everything and call Marcus."

She nodded again. Imaginary Hazel wasn't nearly as talkative as regular Hazel.

Footsteps sounded outside my door. I lifted the corner of the curtain and spotted Hazel. Tears sprang to my eyes. I opened the door wide, and she wrapped me up in a long hug. I didn't want to let go. I wanted to go home with her. When we parted, I tugged her over to sit by me on the bed.

She patted my mattress. "Oh, this is comfy."

"Right? I'm sure I'll miss it when I leave this place."

"Any idea when that will be?" she asked.

I shook my head. I hadn't seen Marcus since he visited me the first day.

"I don't understand why you're here. Peg, you've made the

front page of the newspaper." Hazel shook her head. "It's been awful at home. Reporters are in the street out front. We keep the curtains shut and stay inside. I have to sneak CB out back to do his business."

"Why would reporters be at our house?" I asked.

She shifted on the bed. "Marcus held a press conference late last night."

"What did he say?"

"Well." She chewed on her lip. "He said you were a person of interest in the case."

"Pfft." I tapped my foot. "That man. Why would he do that? He must have had a reason. Did he say where I was?"

"No, didn't even hint about it." She patted my hand.

I rubbed the back of my neck. Marcus was on my last nerve. He'd be getting a phone call soon. "Did you see a guard outside?"

She narrowed her eyes. "No. Should I have?"

"I guess not." I filled her in on how Marcus had tricked me into going to the station. Then I told her my questions about who might have killed Roger and Kurt. "Did you know Kurt's last name was Lynch?" I asked her.

She shook her head.

"Who else has that same last name? It sounds so familiar."

Hazel snapped her fingers. "Karla, that's who. Dr. Harry introduced her way back when we first met her."

"You're right. I do remember now. So, we have ... Wait, did you bring a notebook?"

Hazel winked and pulled one out of her purse. "Of course, I did."

I hugged it to my chest. "I've been keeping notes in my head. Now I can write them down."

"Too bad you can't download them to it." Hazel chuckled.

"Before we start, how are my kids? How's my sweet Reese?

Have you seen Lauree?" It may have only been two days, but I usually saw or talked to my family every day. I could call them from the landline in my room, but I wasn't sure it was safe.

Hazel updated me on the kids. She hadn't seen Lauree but reminded me I hadn't been gone long.

"I'm so worried about her, John, and the kids." I opened the notebook and clicked the pen. "Let me write my thoughts down before you leave. Oh, and can you find out Roger's time of death? That would help my investigation." I spoke as I wrote. "Besides, when he died, have they found Gabby? I'm afraid Stuart might be in danger."

I explained my rationalization based on Gabby and Stuart's relationship. "Or, the two of them could be working together."

"I have a question," Hazel said. "If Estelle is Stuart's great-aunt, Gabby is Stuart's niece, and Kurt was Gabby's stepbrother, where does Karla figure in?"

"Why do you think Karla is part of it?"

"Just think. She and Kurt have the same last name. It's possible, you have to admit."

She was right. Finding that out might help bring this all full circle.

Chapter 22

When she left, Hazel let me keep her notebook and pen. "Here." I tore out my list of questions. "Check on these, please." I hugged her and whispered in her ear, "Be careful. Talk to Marcus and find out why he wanted me sequestered like this. He knows more than he told me."

I sank onto the bed. The relief and excitement I felt when Hazel came left in a rush. I lay down and sniffled. I'd have to wait and see what she found out. Roger's time of death would help defend me if someone decided I should be arrested. I worried about Stuart. He might be in danger from his niece. And who knew if or why Karla was involved?

"Karla!" I sat up straight. Harry said that Karla had told him Cynthia had left. What if Karla shot my daughter with the Rohypnol? I clenched my fists and lay back down. I had no recourse right now. My hands were tied.

After a short nap, I ate another delicious lunch courtesy of the diner and then paced. Pushups and jumping jacks were out, but I could outpace anyone I knew. Going over and over the same questions bored me, so I decided to recite Scriptures and sing praise songs, get my head on straight, and focus on something besides myself. I sat cross-legged on my bed, eyes closed, and hummed, "He's got the whole world in His hands."

Another knock sounded on my door. I waited. "Peg?" asked the same voice from the other day.

"Yes?" I asked.

"I'm here to help you. Come on outside." He rapped the door again.

Nope, not going to open the door. Marcus said he left a guard. He didn't say anything about going somewhere with him. "I'm fine where I am. Tell me how you can help."

"Your detective friend is hiding you." He whistled softly. "Look, I gotta go. Keep me in mind if you want to escape this room." He tapped the door and left.

Hiding me? Why would Marcus do that? He put this guy here to keep me safe, but the man's last words hit me—escape? What did he mean by that?

I lay back on my bed, ankles crossed, arms behind my head. Could I get out of this motel? Marcus took my keys, and the only contact I had with him, Shortie, and Hazel was this old phone. Should I take the guard up on his offer? I sighed. Who would've ever thought I'd be in this situation?

My life—the one I thought I needed to change—had spun out of control. I imagined I needed to wait until all the kids and Hazel moved out, to find happiness. I put myself on hold for years and strained to break free. My eyes grew heavy. I turned on my side. A little nap would help.

My motel room floated in the ocean, and quetzals fluttered

around it. A soft breeze ruffled the birds' feathers. One of them squeezed through the crack under the door and settled on my bed. Its large, dark eyes fixed on me.

"Can I help you?" it asked.

"Yes, I want to leave here." I stroked its beautiful feathers.

"Sorry, can't do that. You'll be here for a while." The bird morphed into my guard. I jerked back my hand.

"Hi, Peg. Sorry, I can't help you either." The man, a dark figure with his face blotted out, leaned closer.

I scrambled to the corner of my room. "I'm not supposed to be in here." I reached out, and something hard brushed against my hand. I picked it up and showed it to the man.

He laughed. "You gonna murder me like you did Roger Keaton and Kurt?"

"I didn't kill anyone." My words came out in a hiss. I looked at my hand, which was filled with coins. "How would I hurt someone with these?"

He turned into Stuart, who wore a dive mask and stuck his head in the water. He came up spluttering. "Gabby borrowed this without asking." He shoved the mask to the top of his head. "You have to escape and help me. I'm in danger. Then we can find more coins—you, me, and Gabby."

I woke with a gasp, my hair matted with sweat. Gabby and Stuart. Hazel's phone call with Stuart. I forgot to ask her what he said. He could be in danger from his niece. I was more convinced now than ever. The hair on the back of my neck stood up straight, and goosebumps broke out down my arms.

Where was Marcus? I'd been here two days, and no one besides Shortie and Hazel had visited. I had questions that needed to be answered.

I washed my face and finger-combed my damp hair. I was about to go buy a soda when someone knocked on my door. "Please be Marcus," I whispered.

"Hi, Peggy." The guard was back.

I sighed. "Hi. Why are you here?" Again.

"Come with me." He rattled the doorknob.

"Marcus told me to stay here. He'll come get me when it's time."

"Oh, yeah. That's why I'm here." He cleared his throat. "Come on, girl." His voice sounded desperate.

I jerked open my door. He stepped back and waved me out. I studied his face. I'd never seen this person before.

What should I do? Should I trust him like Marcus did? I rushed back for my notebook. "Fine." I stopped a foot away from him. "You're sure Marcus said I should go with you?"

"Yes." He smiled.

My gut screamed warnings. I studied his eyes.

He tipped a pretend hat. "Look, we need to go." He grabbed my hand, and we took off down the outside walkway. From the street, a siren screamed.

I pulled away from him. "Is that siren for us?" I wanted to vomit.

"Of course not, honey." He put his hand on the small of my back. "Keep moving."

Now I knew something was wrong. I couldn't imagine a police officer would call me 'honey.' "What do you mean?" We rounded a corner to the back of the motel.

"Go, go, go." He pushed me forward, turned, and ran the other way. He was gone. That rat. Someone tapped my shoulder, and I whipped around, fists raised. I wasn't going down without a fight.

"Peg, come on. We have to hurry." Hazel held out her hand, and once again, I ran. We hopped in her Bug. She tore out of the parking lot, taking a sharp right at the stop sign, away from the direction the police were heading.

"What are we doing? Who told you to come for me? What

is going on?" I had so many questions. My whole world had tipped upside down. Again.

Hazel shook her head. Sweat dripped down her face. "I don't know. I went outside for the mail and found a note in the mailbox. It told me when and where to park and where to wait for you." She panted and fanned herself. "It's been a long time since I ran anywhere."

"Take a breath. Can we pull over? Did the note say where to go?"

Hazel pulled into a parking lot and motored behind a large dumpster. She turned off the engine, took several deep breaths, and released them slowly. "Okay, that's better. Here. You can read it." She reached into her purse.

I smoothed the wrinkled paper. In block print, someone had written the date, time, and place for her to park and meet me. I turned the paper over, but it was blank. "Who put this in our mailbox?"

She held up her palms. "No idea."

"But you came anyway." I hugged her as well as I could in the confined space. I folded the note and handed it back to her. The tiny Bug was bigger than my motel room. I rolled the window down. "Smell that? That's the smell of freedom." I sniffed deeply.

"I think it's trash."

"Oh, no, it's the best." And it was. I didn't know who just helped me escape the motel—no way was it Marcus's guard— but being confined had taught me one thing—I was content with who I was. I struggled so hard to find my happiness and settle into something that made me feel complete, and all the time, I already was. I had God, which was huge. Not everyone had Him. I had my amazing family and friends and a mother-in-law who wouldn't leave me stuck away by myself. Even though I was afraid of losing Lauree, no one, not even death, would take our friendship.

I didn't have to wait to be fulfilled. I didn't have to chase anything. I was happy and free. I leaned back in my seat and relaxed. My eyes drifted shut, a smile spreading over my face.

"Ready to head home?" Hazel asked.

I nodded and sat up. "Yes, I am." I had no idea what or who waited there for me. For all I knew, it might be Marcus or the anonymous caller. She started the car and glanced in the rearview mirror, preparing to back up. At the same time, tires screeched into the parking lot.

"Uh-oh." She revved the engine, whipped the Bug backward, and shot toward the road with a spin of the steering wheel. "Hold on, Peg," she shouted as we bumped off the curb into traffic.

I looked behind us. A black sedan held steady on our tail.

"I think that's Estelle's car. Can we go faster?" The car would hit Hazel's VW any minute.

"I'm trying. Oh, no!" Hazel pointed.

The light up ahead turned red. What to do? I scanned the intersection. "Punch it, Hazel!"

We zoomed through the red light, but the sedan had to stop while traffic crossed. Hazel and I whooped in triumph. She crossed onto Davis Highway, and we headed home. It was impossible to hide her bright yellow Bug. We would hope that Estelle or her driver wouldn't find us.

Hazel turned into our subdivision. As we passed the first road to the right, a black car flashed its headlights. We were trapped.

"I thought we passed them. How did they beat us here?" I wriggled around in my seat and looked behind us.

Hazel checked her rearview mirror. "Yep, you're right. I

can't speed in the neighborhood, though." She curved to the right toward my house.

"Don't stop. Don't stop." I grasped her arm.

"I won't!" She peeled my hand off of her forearm. "I have to drive."

"Sorry. Oh, wait. The car pulled into my driveway." I turned to Hazel, who stepped on the brakes. "We have to go back. What if Cynthia and Carter are home?"

"No one's hurting my grandkids," she growled. She shifted into reverse and sped backward, screeching to a halt at the curb in front of the house. "Come on, Peg."

She clutched her purse and was out of the car and marching down the hill before I unbuckled. Two people, dressed head to toe in black, swooped in and captured her. They dragged her toward the sedan.

"Wait a minute." I rushed around the Bug toward them. "Don't you hurt her. Help! We need help!" I hollered, praying someone would call the police.

I reached them and tried to pull Hazel out of their grip. "Let. Her. Go." I tugged and twisted, but they wouldn't release her. On my next try, I pulled on one of their black balaclavas, and it moved. "It's you!"

"Peg, watch out!"

Hazel's scream penetrated my brain a second too late. I felt a sharp pinch in my neck, and then, nothing.

Chapter 23

My head hurt. I tried to open my eyes, but they were so heavy. Voices. People were speaking, and I recognized one of them. I was supposed to remember something. Someone. A face? Eyes? Yes, eyes. I shifted and groaned at the pain that split through my head.

"She's waking up," a gruff voice said.

"Give her more."

That's the one. I knew that voice. It belonged to someone I cared about. Confusion filled me before another pinch. Darkness fell again.

Blinding light forced me to open my eyes. "What is that? Turn it off!"

A click sounded, and darkness enveloped me.

"Peg, *psst*, Peg. Don't go back to sleep."

I recognized Hazel's voice. I opened my eyes in a squint. "Hazel, where are we? What happened?" I tried to move, but the pain in my head stopped me.

She exhaled. "I'm so glad you're okay. We're at the Center. They brought us here."

Another click, and dim light surrounded us. I blinked several times, and my vision cleared. I could hardly see her. She held a flashlight down by her side.

"What happened?" I examined the room. We were in Dr. Harry's internal office. "How'd we end up here? Ugh, my head is killing me."

"They took us, and they shot you with some kind of drug." Her voice wobbled.

"I remember. It hurt. The rest is a blank." I struggled to lift my hands. "I can't move."

"Me either," she whispered. She turned the small flashlight with her fingers so I could see better. We were tied to wooden chairs in the center of the room, facing each other.

"Where did you find that?" I tipped my head to the light.

"They didn't take my purse, and I keep one in it. I was able to fish it out."

My mother-in-law—always prepared. Warmth filled me.

"I'm in here too." Dr. Harry's voice came from my left, Hazel's right.

I gasped, my heart beating triple time. Hazel jerked the flashlight his way. He sat on the floor in the corner, hands and feet bound with a thick rope. Blood trickled down his forehead.

"When did you get in here? Are you okay?" I asked.

He lowered his gaze. "I was in my office checking on ..."

"We know about the eggs, Harry." Disgust laced Hazel's words.

His body slumped. "They do, too, apparently. They hit me on the head and tied me up in here. I overheard them talking. They plan to sell the eggs and buy more gold coins." He sniffled.

"You're crying over bird eggs?" I could not believe I ever found this man attractive.

He raised his bound hands and wiped his nose on his sleeve. "Yes, I am, and I'm not afraid to admit it. I was researching how to breed quetzals. And I did it. I'm the one who got those birds to lay more eggs."

I thought the birds took care of that part.

He continued. "I met with those nasty Keatons." He shivered. "Now, the quetzals won't be endangered." His eyes, reflected in Hazel's flashlight, glimmered with pride.

"That was a noble gesture," I said, not being snarky. He had attempted to save a species. "How did the Keatons contact you? Did they say they had a quetzal?"

"They had two of them. At first, I received a letter in the mail, so I came to Pensacola."

Hazel wriggled in her chair. "Can we talk about this later? I need the little girls' room." She tried to pull her hands through the rope that bound her, but it didn't budge.

"Hang on. I have a utility knife in here. I didn't think about it before." Harry managed to wiggle to his knees and scooch toward a shelf. He found the knife and knee-shuffled to Hazel. "I think I can cut through the ropes."

"Be careful," she said through gritted teeth. She winced as he sawed.

"Be still," he grouched. "This isn't easy."

"Not on my end either." Hazel squinched her eyes shut.

"Is he hurting you?" I gritted my teeth, hoping he wouldn't cut her.

"No, I'm just waiting for him to slip," she said.

"Hang on, here we go." The ropes came off one of Hazel's hands. "Ta-da!" Harry said.

She held out her now free hand. "Give me that. I'll do my other hand."

"You're welcome." He handed her the knife.

Hazel freed herself, then me, and lastly, she cut Harry's ropes. She looked at the door. "Do you think they're still out there?"

Harry shook his head. "They were making plans. They're long gone by now. But—" His eyes twinkled in the dim light. "My boat is outside."

Hazel and I ducked into the restroom before joining Harry out back. The sun began its descent, and soft colors filled the sky. Around us, birds preened, and frogs croaked. A gentle breeze fluttered through my hair, like any ordinary summer evening. But nothing about this day was normal.

We climbed in the front of his boat, and Harry started the motor.

"Wait a minute," I shouted above the noise.

"What?" he said.

"Where are we going?" We couldn't take off. We needed to tell someone what had happened or call the police. I remembered the person who helped get me away from the motel. I still didn't know if Marcus sent him.

"We have to find those birds and the eggs." Harry steered us into the bayou and headed for open water.

I leaned toward Hazel. "No one knows where we are. Do we trust Harry?" I had so many questions. "Who sent you the note to find me outside of the motel? Did Estelle set that up?" A memory floated through my mind. I shook my head. "There's something I can't think of, Hazel. Someone I saw."

"I thought I recognized one of the voices of the people who grabbed us," she said.

Familiar voices struck a nerve. "Was it Estelle?"

She pursed her lips and shook her head. "I don't think so. I'm not sure I'd recognize her voice. It was someone else." She tapped her head. "Steel trap up here, but it's not letting the right stuff out."

I knew how she felt. I was still woozy from whatever I'd been given. We knew Harry wasn't involved in our abduction. He was a victim himself. Unless Estelle said, "Birds alive!" I didn't think I'd know her voice either. Roger was dead. So was Kurt. Who else could it be?

"Was it Gabby? Karla? Those are the only two I can think of." I snapped my fingers. "What about Stuart?"

"I don't know. I just don't." Her shoulders slumped.

"What did Stuart say when you talked to him the other day? The day Marcus sent me to the motel? Remember, you were on the phone with him when I left."

She opened her mouth to respond when Harry announced, "We're here." The boat bumped a dock, and he shut down the motor.

"Where are we?" I accepted his hand to step onto the dock and waited while he helped Hazel out of the boat.

Harry wiggled his eyebrows. "Blue Oyster Marina. I live here. There's probably not many people here this time of day, but I think I know someone who can help us discover who kidnapped us."

"Who?" I asked.

We fell into step beside him, heading toward the deck where we first met the members of the Pensacola branch of the Society for Shipwrecks. He gestured to some chairs.

"Why don't you two relax? We've been through a lot. I'll go inside and find someone to help."

Hazel and I collapsed into our seats. She moaned, and I massaged my neck until a thought stopped me cold.

"Do you have your phone?" I asked her.

She patted her purse. "Of course."

I blinked.

Her mouth dropped open. "Oh, my."

"Yeah." I held out my hand.

She fished inside her bag and handed me the cell with a sheepish expression. "Never even crossed my mind."

"It's okay. I didn't think of it until right now." I dialed Marcus's number and tapped the speaker button. "He's going to be mad at me."

Marcus answered with a grunt. "Hazel? Do you happen to know where your darling daughter-in-law is?"

"Hi, Marcus, it's me."

Harry stepped back onto the deck, Stuart in tow. "Look who I found."

"Stuart? What's going on? Why were we kidnapped?"

Marcus hollered my name, but I ignored him.

Stuart crossed his arms. "I don't have any idea what you're talking about."

"That's not him," Hazel stage whispered.

"Nope." That wasn't the voice I remembered, either, but it sounded vaguely familiar. "Stuart, where are Ted and Gabby?"

"How should I know?" He shrugged like a sulky teenager.

The door from the building to the deck opened, and my blood ran cold. Hazel gasped. It couldn't be. I didn't believe it until he spoke.

"Hi, Peg, Hazel. Nice of you all to join us." The man's smile, one I never thought of as smarmy before, didn't reach his eyes.

I knew those eyes and his voice—that's the memory that eluded me. I never expected to see him take a gun out of his multi-pocket birding vest and point it toward us.

"I remember now. I pulled off your balaclava." My stomach churned. Owen—sweet, kind Owen who helped me pick out the best shoes for birding, led us on trips, and who Hazel had a crush on—was involved in our abduction. The gun in his hand made everything too real.

"Sorry about that. You weren't supposed to see me." Owen pulled out a chair and sat. He waved the gun at Stuart and Harry. "Come join us, please, gentlemen."

Hazel's phone lay on the table. I shifted my hand to keep it out of Owen's sight and pressed the speaker button off.

"Owen Walters, why would you do this?" Marcus would know who had us. Now to tell him where we were.

Owen chuckled and shook his head as if I were stupid. "Money, of course. You saw how Margaret reacted. Dr. Turnball, such a good friend, but clueless." He leaned toward me. "Who do you think started those rumors about the coins? I needed a little coin myself. Get it? Coin? Coins?"

I didn't know this Owen. The gentle, retired history professor. He used all of us, even his old friend Margaret. Nausea joined the churning.

"How do the quetzals figure in?" I asked.

He waved the gun in the air. "That's all Estelle. Gabby, that guy's niece— " He aimed the firearm at Stuart. "She set it all up."

Hazel sat beside me, frozen. I reached out my hand and covered hers. "Are you okay?" I whispered.

She turned her hand over and gripped mine. She squeezed it three times. Then, with a gasp, she yelled, "Owen Walters, I was in love with you." She burst into loud sobs. In between breaths, she said, "How could you? How could you? You, of all people. And here at the Blue Oyster Marina. Why, Owen, why?"

I nibbled on the inside of my cheek to keep from smiling. This woman continued to amaze me. She knew the phone was on, and she'd just told Marcus where we were. In the midst of this craziness, she came through. I squeezed her hand back three times. *I. Love. You.* I was sure some of her tears were real. Owen had broken both of our hearts.

Owen stood. "We're not staying here, dear. Come on, everyone up. We'll use your boat, Doc."

Harry's face paled. "Um ... I'm not sure we can fit—all five of us. How about you leave the women behind?"

His gallant gesture touched me.

"Sorry, no, I'm not doing that. We'll be fine. Let's go. We have a trip to make over to the Fort." He waved us to go in front of him.

I pocketed Hazel's cell, hoping Marcus could still hear. "We're going to Fort Pickens?" I asked as I passed him.

Owen touched my back. "Yes, Peg. Back to where this all started."

I knew what he meant. Back to where we found Roger Keaton.

Dead.

Chapter 24

We squished into Harry's boat. Owen sat between Hazel and me while Stuart balanced on his heels near the front. Harry started the motor and headed for Pensacola Bay.

The marina disappeared from my sight. Not one person observed what happened. I'd never seen the place so empty. I also never imagined I'd sit by Owen while he held a gun. The world had gone mad.

"Did I tell you about Lauree?" I thought I might reach the kind man I once knew. "She has breast cancer. It's so bad. She might not make it."

Hazel patted his leg. "Remember her from our first meeting? She's Peg's best friend. They say she might not live much longer. I can't imagine."

Owen reached down with his non-gun hand and removed her hand from his leg. "Don't touch me."

Hazel sat back, arms crossed. She huffed. "How did you fake it so long? Being nice, Owen. That's what I want you to tell me."

He drew a deep breath and exhaled slowly. "I wasn't faking it. Not really."

"Not at first, you mean?" My anger toward him grew by the second. I didn't feel sorry for him. No way.

"No. You're right. I'm sorry, Peg." He turned his sad blue gaze my way.

I gritted my teeth. *Stay strong*, I told myself. *He isn't the man you thought he was.* I looked away before my feelings took a physical form.

"Listen. My wife died. I told you that, right?"

Hazel and I nodded.

He shifted on the hard seat. I hoped he was uncomfortable. Right now, I hoped lots of bad things happened to him. Some long, thick splinters stabbing his legs for starters.

The fort drew closer. I didn't know what he would do when we arrived, so I nudged him. "And?"

"I didn't have any money left. Our insurance didn't cover all her treatments. I needed some money and quickly. I don't make much in retirement, after all."

His whining irritated me. "My husband died. Hazel's husband died. You don't see us kidnapping people and stealing old coins."

"You don't understand." He shook his head, pain lining his face. "No one does. I loved my wife more than life. She should have never died."

His 'why me' attitude stomped on my last nerve.

"My husband was young when he died. He didn't have the chance to see his kids grow up or meet his grandchild. Don't talk to me about your problems." My lip curled. It wasn't a good idea to irritate him, but I also wanted to catch him off guard. Use his emotions to make him misstep if possible.

Harry pulled close to a sandy beach area. I recognized it from when we found the blue tarp the same day Hazel discovered Roger Keaton's body. Just over the brick wall stood Fort Pickens. I prayed Marcus had heard enough of the conversation to know where to find us. Just in case, I said, "I remember this place. Do you, Hazel? We found the tarp here." I turned to Owen. "Did you kill Roger Keaton too?"

He stared at me, his eyes flat and hard. "Estelle and Gabby."

Okay, then. That answered that.

"This close enough?" Harry asked.

"Perfect." Owen waved the gun. "Pull up here. Everyone out. Come on, hurry." He checked his watch. "They'll be here soon."

We climbed over the side into shin-deep water and trudged out of it onto the sand.

"Who's coming?" I prayed Marcus could still hear us.

"My team." Owen gestured us closer to the wall.

Harry pulled his boat up on the beach, and the four of us huddled together. Owen approached, the setting sun backlighting his body.

What were my children doing? Did they know we were in trouble or think I was still in hiding? What about Lauree? I wanted to see my friend again. Hug her and find out if there were options for her treatment. And be available to help John and the kids.

I drew a slow, steady breath, pointed behind Owen, and yelled, "Look!" When he turned, I squatted and grabbed two fistfuls of sand. "Hey, Owen?"

He turned back to me and stepped closer, a confused expression on his face. "What?"

"Here." I threw the sand in his eyes and hollered, "Run!" We had already run today, and this time, our shoes were wet and clogged with sand. I didn't think I could take much more, and I was sure Hazel was spent. When we got out of this, we might take up jogging.

"We need to start exercising," she gasped, mirroring my thoughts.

"Come on, we don't have time to talk." I tried to go faster, but she slowed and breathed hard. I glanced back to find Owen closing the gap.

A grunt came from behind us, and I chanced another look. Stuart had fallen in the sand, and Owen tripped over him. The two men grappled.

Harry hollered, "Come on, let's head for that part of the fort." He pointed.

"The gift shop will be closed," I panted. Hazel slowed again, and I urged her on. "Just a little more. We can hide inside the fort. Don't stop now."

We passed under the archway and hooked a left into the former quarters. I remembered our tour, led at the time by our now-former friend. "Owen said Geronimo didn't have his own cell, but there were spaces back here we never explored. I think we can find somewhere to hide."

Harry gave me a thumbs-up and darted down several of the side areas. He shook his head every time he came out until he went in and didn't come out. From a distance, he called Hazel and me.

"Can we trust him?" I leaned over, hands on my knees, and tried to catch my breath.

Hazel shrugged and walked forward down the shallow steps. "I don't think we have a choice."

Owen shouted my name somewhere behind me. Hazel was right. Our choice, limited as it was, was to go with Harry.

And pray.

I caught up to Hazel, who murmured to herself. She raised her eyebrows. "I'm not crazy; I'm just praying."

We were on the same page again. We ducked under a low entrance and emerged into a large, round area. The bricks here were lighter and resembled an off-white plaster. Up ahead, Harry waved. We hurried to him.

"I found another section I think we can hide in. Follow me." He shined his cell phone flashlight, and we traipsed behind him until we hit a dead end.

"Should we circle back and find another place?" Hazel asked.

He shook his head and clicked off the light. "I don't think so. Let's huddle in here. I hope Stuart got away from Owen and can call for help. There's no cell service in here."

We sat for what felt like hours. Any shift in position echoed throughout our space. We didn't talk, afraid the noise would travel. Owen's voice and several others occasionally reached us, but none came very close.

"How long have we been in here?" I assumed we had spent at least several hours by now.

Harry touched his cell phone's screen. "When we got in here, it was after seven. Now it's nine-thirty."

I thought we'd been waiting longer. Hours longer. "Think they're gone? I can't believe Marcus isn't here."

Hazel gasped. "What if he came? We've stayed here, and he might have arrested Owen by now. We have to investigate and search for Stuart. Turn on your light, Harry."

He did. She stood and brushed off her pants. "Let's go look." She took off, ducking under the overhang.

Harry and I exchanged looks, shrugged, and followed her.

After a few wrong turns, we found the entrance. Harry volunteered to peek outside, and he wasn't gone long.

"No one's in the parking lot. I didn't see Stuart either, but I think we can make it to my boat." He grinned, and his dimple flashed.

I ignored it. I had to. This wasn't the time for dimples. We needed to leave before Owen and his team returned.

We made our way back to Harry's boat, the moon lighting our path. I pointed to a section of disturbed sand.

"I think that's where Stuart fell."

"I hope he's okay," Hazel said. "Even though he was strange, I don't wish anything bad on him."

We learned today that strange didn't equal evil. Owen kept up a pretense for months. We trusted him and thought he was one of the good guys.

"Do you think Estelle got to Owen?" I asked.

"He knew she and Gabby killed Roger. Probably Kurt too." Hazel sniffled. "I keep thinking about Owen. I underestimated him." She wiped her cheeks.

I put my arm around her shoulders. "We all did. We had no reason to believe he was anything but what he showed us. He deceived us all."

Harry waved us toward his boat. "It's still here. Let's go."

"Thank God," I said. We needed to get home. I needed to lay down my guilt over Anna and Sylvia's deaths and attribute them to the real criminal—Estelle. She, along with Gabby and Owen, committed the crimes this time. They shot Roger, killed Kurt, and kidnapped Hazel and me, and then Harry and Stuart. All of these were their responsibility, and they needed to pay for their offenses.

What I realized when I left the motel held true. I had everything I needed. I didn't have to be available every second for my kids. They didn't need me like they used to. While that was a bit of a punch to the gut, it was true. The one question I still had was where I stood with Shortie. When I got home, I'd figure that out. Right now, we had to get there safely.

Harry sped across the bay and motored up Bayou Chico to the Center. Hazel and I disembarked and waited for him to secure the boat. We would drop him at the Blue Oyster Marina and head home.

I couldn't wait to sleep in my own bed.

We got to the parking lot, and all three of us stopped dead in our tracks.

"My Bug isn't here," Hazel said.

I groaned. No, it wasn't. We had left it parked at the curb in front of my house. "Harry, do you have a car at the Marina?"

He nodded, and we tromped back to his boat.

"What if Owen shows up?" Hazel said.

"He hasn't caught us yet. We won't borrow trouble." Trouble followed us, but so far, no Owen. No Marcus, either, and I didn't understand that. I fished Hazel's cell from my pocket. "Here, does this still have power?"

She turned it on, and it dinged with text after text. "Uh-oh, Marcus is mad. Oh, Peg—" She slapped her hand over her mouth and spoke through her fingers. "You might be going to jail. He said so. Or prison. See?"

She handed me the phone, and I scrolled through Marcus's messages, each one angrier than the one before. Apparently, the guy who helped me 'escape' wasn't his guy, after all. I gave the cell phone back to her.

"Nothing I could do. Marcus could have kept me informed. I think Estelle set me up with the guy who came to my motel room."

"And that note I got?" Hazel pulled it out of her purse and waved it in the air. "I still have it—proof, I think."

"Right. Don't lose that. Hopefully, Marcus heard part of Owen's confession."

Hazel turned to me. "But Peg, why didn't he come?"

That was a good question.

Chapter 25

There were no other messages besides Marcus's texts. My phone was somewhere in a nasty, trash-filled dumpster, and my car was at the police station, and Marcus had my keys. Had Shortie tried to find me today? How were my kids? I imagined they were frightened with Hazel's car parked at the curb but their grandmother nowhere in sight. What if Owen went to my house? Cynthia knew him and thought he was a friend—one of the harmless birders. Hazel hadn't been able to get hold of her to warn her.

We arrived at the Marina. Harry tied up his boat, helped us out, and we hurried to his car. I gave him directions to my house and held my breath until we arrived. He slowed down when we reached my subdivision.

"Should we park down the street? Approach on foot?" He sounded more like Marcus than himself.

"Good idea. There's an empty lot over here. Pull up by the curb." I had him turn the car around, nose out, in case we needed to leave quickly.

The neighborhood was quiet, as it should be at this time of night or morning. We walked toward my house. I didn't see anyone nearby. No strange cars or black sedans. I didn't want to be abducted again. Hazel's Bug sat at the curb.

"I don't have my keys." I stopped. "Do you smell gasoline?"

Hazel and Harry sniffed the air.

"Yeah, I do." Harry walked to the side of the house. "It's back here too."

Hazel reached into her purse. "I have my keys. Let's go in and call the police. Probably the neighbors gassed up their boat." She unlocked the front door, and we hurried inside. She flipped the lock behind us. "We have got to invest in a good security system, Peg."

"Yes, you do."

My heart stopped, and we froze. The words and the voice. I knew them. I flipped on the light and screamed. Carter and Cynthia sat on the couch, duct tape over their mouths and rope tied around their hands and ankles. Owen stood by the back sliding door, gun aimed at us, Gabby by his side.

"Come in, come in." He waved us to the sofa.

I burrowed between my kids and hugged them, whispering, "I love you," into their ears. Hazel and Harry squished beside each other on Carter's other side.

"Can I at least take the tape off their mouths?" My words came out in a growl. He had messed with my kids, and this mamma bear wasn't having any of it.

"Sure. Gabby?"

Gabby ripped it off in one go. "Less pain this way."

Carter hollered, but Cynthia started talking as soon as the tape was removed.

"He's supposed to be a good birder. You told me. I let him in even though it was late. I hoped he knew where you two were." Tears streamed down her cheeks.

"It's okay. I thought he was a friend too." I turned to the two kidnappers. "Where is CB?"

"My dog." Hazel stood. "Where is my dog, Charlie Brown?"

Owen sneered. "He came right to me. I gave him a biscuit, and he's napping in the back room."

Hazel raised her fists and stomped her foot. "You better not have hurt him. How could I have believed in you? You ... you traitor!" She plopped back on the couch and hid her face against Carter's shoulder.

"Where's Estelle?" I asked.

Owen shrugged. "She left after we looked for you at the fort. Anyhow, I don't need her to find more coins. She only cares about the stupid birds." He narrowed his eyes. "Dr. Harry, how did you find the coins?"

"Estelle gave them to me. She brought me the two quetzals and a handful of coins. I stuck them on the shelf in my extra office. My interest is in the birds, not some dirty old coins." He spit out the words.

The muscles in Owen's cheeks twitched. "Those dirty old coins are much more valuable than birds." His tone indicated his real feelings about birding.

"That may be what you think." Harry's stuffy, know-it-all attitude was on full display.

"I'm surprised the police didn't find you." What happened to Marcus? Why hadn't he found us?

Gabby wiggled her eyebrows. "I took care of that."

"What did you do?" I raised my voice. "Did you hurt Marcus?"

"Calm down, Peg. Gabby started ... well, let's just say she started a small conflagration."

Fire? Marcus wasn't a firefighter. "Where?"

"At the police station," Gabby sing-songed, twirling her hair around her finger. "Right where I could trap him."

Hazel shifted on the couch. "I have a question. How does Karla figure into this?"

"Aunt Karla? She's not any part of it." She hooked her arm through Owen's. "It's just me and this old guy."

Owen glared at her until she let him go. He brushed off his arm.

"Okay, wait a minute. Karla's last name is Lynch," I said. "She's your aunt?"

"Yep."

"Why did you think Karla would hurt anyone?" Harry leaned forward to ask me.

"She acted like she didn't like me." I figured it all wrong.

He snorted. "She was jealous, that's all. She thought I would take her away and teach her about birds. We would sail off into the sunset." He shook his head. "I don't even have a sailboat."

The man was clueless, but he wasn't evil like Owen. "Who killed Kurt?"

"I did," Gabby teared up. "I loved him. He was a good stepbrother and even got me a job at the Center. Great-aunt Estelle said he had to go. So, whack." The tears stopped, and she imitated hitting him in the head.

My mouth dropped open. She was insane. "Great-aunt Estelle?"

"Yep." Gabby picked up the rope off my dining table and handed Owen several pieces. "You tie up Dr. Harry. I'll do the women."

"Yep ... and?" I prompted.

She tied my ankles. "She's my dad's aunt. My grandma's sister." She motioned for me to hold out my hands and started on my wrists.

"Why kill Roger?" I asked. I held my wrists apart as far as possible.

She shrugged. Her nonchalance and indifference scared me. She had zero sense of right and wrong.

"Estelle again. She said he got in her way, and she was bored with him."

Owen chuckled. "She wanted all the money to herself is more like it." He finished tying Harry and stepped back, keeping his gun trained on us. "Hurry up, Gabby. We need to leave. The fire won't keep that cop for long."

"Detective," I said. "He's a detective, and we'll tell him what you told us." I shook my finger at him. "You will be captured, Owen Walters."

Gabby held up a lighter and flicked on the flame. "I think we can get away just fine."

Now I knew what the gasoline was for.

It's true your life flashes before your eyes when it's about to end. My life, all the what-ifs, my kids' lives, my sweet grandbaby Reese, Marcus, my BFF Lauree—all that zoomed through my mind. I was not going down this way, and neither were my loved ones. Not even Dr. Harry.

Owen and Gabby darted through the sliding glass door, and there was a click—the lighter. Panic tore through me, and I sucked in a breath.

"Come on. We have to leave. The fire will spread quickly."

"Mom," Carter said, "I have a knife in my pocket. Can you reach it?" He leaned toward his grandmother, and I worked my tied hands into his pants pocket.

"Thank God you have this with you." I worked on the ropes around his hands, and he cut us all free. The gasoline odor grew stronger, and flames licked up the back deck.

"Oh, Peg, how can we get out?" Hazel held onto my arm.

Whoosh. I turned at the noise. The front porch railing had caught fire. My house was brick, but they managed to hedge us in by the front and back doors. The kids could shimmy out through a window, but I wasn't sure Hazel would be able to. I wouldn't leave her behind.

"Hazel, call Marcus. Leave a message if you have to. Carter, call nine-one-one and take Roscoe. Cynthia, find some towels, and we'll wet them down."

"How can I help?" Harry rubbed his hands together.

"Find CB. He's in one of the bedrooms." Poor Charlie Brown, once again the victim of the bad guy. "Can you carry him?"

"Sure." He returned to the kitchen with the Weimaraner in his arms, grunted, and shifted his hands. "Let's go."

Cynthia stood at the sink, squeezing extra water from several towels. She handed one to each of us and turned to me. "How are we getting out, Mom? We can't use the front or back door."

I'd thought about that. "The garage. There's trim around it, but not on the ground. Throw the towel over your head."

We gathered in the garage, and I pushed the button to raise the door. I didn't have time to mourn my little house. We had to escape.

"Go, go, go!" I waved them past Carter's car and through the opening. "Go right and head down the street."

Carter held out Roscoe's cage. "Take this, I'll warn Ms. Lauree."

My sweet kid. Always thinking about others. I nodded, took the birdcage, and helped Hazel. The last two days of constant adventure and no sleep had caught up to her. She stumbled as she walked. We stopped at the corner by Harry's car and turned to see the fire spread up and over my house. I cringed at the awful creaking and crackling noises. The sound of sirens up the road renewed my hope. Maybe they'd arrive before the place was destroyed.

Carter trotted toward us. "Mr. John is taking Ms. Lauree and the twins the other way down the street. He's worried the wind will blow sparks on their house."

Good thinking. I hadn't noticed the wind, but dark, menacing clouds gathered instead of a pretty summer sunrise. Lightning shot through them, and I jumped when thunder boomed. It had been days since I'd checked the weather. And since I slept.

I drew a deep breath. How would this end? "Hazel, did you contact Marcus?"

Hazel sat on the curb, elbows on her knees, and watched the house burn. I squatted in front of her and caught her gaze.

"Are you okay?"

Her eyes sparkled with unshed tears. She wiped them, her hand shaking. "Yes." Her words came out in a whisper. "Know what I was thinking?"

"No, what?"

She tipped her head, a sad smile lifting her lips. "My house hasn't sold. At least we have a place to go."

"Yeah." I didn't want to think that far ahead. "Did Marcus answer when you called?"

She shook her head. "I left a message."

"I wonder where Stuart is? Owen didn't mention him."

Two firetrucks barreled toward us. I didn't have to show them where to go. By now, my house was engulfed in flames, and the roof would catch soon. I sank onto the curb beside my mother-in-law.

"He won. That evil man won." I covered my face.

"Don't forget Estelle," Hazel said.

I leaned my head on her shoulder and cried.

Chapter 26

When it was all over, my roof looked intact. The whole house would have to be inspected before we could go in, not to mention repairing the smoke and water damage. We were soaked head to toe, but the storm helped stop the blaze from spreading. Lauree invited us to change at her house, where she passed out shorts and T-shirts.

I held up the sundress she handed me. "Pink polka dots? That's the best you have?"

"Short notice, but better than the soaked clothes you had on. It's too big on me now anyhow." Her lips trembled. "What happened, Peg? How did the fire start? John said he smelled gasoline."

What should I tell her? I didn't want to burden her with more right now. Her health was so bad, and what I told her would increase her stress. Our presence might mean she and her family were at risk. Marcus still hadn't responded to Hazel's texts and voicemails, so he couldn't give me guidance.

"I don't want to tell you too much. Trust me, Lauree. Thank you for all the help, but we need to leave."

She stepped closer and put her hands on my shoulders. "Be careful, please."

I promised her I would. As careful as possible. She and John volunteered to keep CB and Roscoe, and we left. Carter drove Hazel's Bug, and Harry followed in his car.

When we arrived at her old house, Hazel collapsed on the sofa. I urged her to go sleep in her room, but she insisted on a shower first. Her bedroom door clicked shut, and I sighed.

Carter and Cynthia both had worried expressions. "Grandma's gonna be all right, right, Mom?" Carter's voice carried all the hurt of the night.

"I think so." I hugged them tight and thanked God we were safe and had a place to stay.

"Does Owen know where Hazel's house is?" Harry asked.

"I don't see how. He met her at my house. He might know she once had a different place, but he probably wouldn't know she still owned it." I leaned against the kitchen counter. "Want to hear something ironic?"

The three of them nodded. Dirt streaked Harry's face, and I leaned forward and wiped it off. Despite being closer to my age, he reminded me of my kids—young and still learning. Book smart didn't equal maturity.

"The roof on this house was just repaired from Hurricane Hazel. That's not ironic, though. That's all God."

SOMEHOW I SLEPT the rest of the day and into the next morning. I woke up hungry and irritable. I bowed my head and thanked God for the blessings and the help He'd already provided. It was a miracle no one had been hurt in the house fire, and I added that to my thanks. Prayer improved my attitude.

Someone left clothes outside my bedroom door. They

looked like Hazel's, but I refused to complain. It was better than pink polka dots. I showered in the hall bathroom and got dressed. As I headed for the kitchen, I tossed Lauree's polka-dot dress on the washer.

"Food, I need food. And coffee." I greeted my kids and Harry. "Where's Grandma?"

"She went to Lauree's to pick up the bird and the dog," Harry said.

Carter poured coffee and handed it to me. He kissed my cheek. "She loves those animals."

The first sip hit the spot. I had a lot of work ahead of me—sifting through my house when they allowed me to, dealing with insurance, figuring out where we would live. I closed my eyes and enjoyed a moment of quiet.

The front door opened, ending my peaceful time. CB bounded in, no worse for wear after our traumatic experience. He received lots of love and pats. Roscoe chirped, but he didn't volunteer any new words. Hazel set his cage on the hearth.

"Harry, can you help me?" she asked.

The two returned with three boxes of donuts.

"That's a lot of sugar." I opened one box. My mouth watered, and my stomach growled. "Never mind. It'll take all of these to satisfy us today."

"I thought so." Hazel brought plates and napkins to the table. "Dig in. I knew I only had coffee in the house, and we deserve a little lift today."

"Cynthia and I can go buy groceries later," Carter mumbled around his donut.

"Good idea," Hazel said with a frown. "Still no word from Marcus."

Why hadn't he answered her calls and texts? My mouth went dry with fear, and I choked on my bite of donut.

"Mom?" Cynthia picked off a piece of apple fritter and

nibbled on it. "What about Shortie? You haven't mentioned him. Does he know what happened?"

Her comment stopped me in my tracks. I worried about Marcus, and Shortie didn't even cross my mind until she mentioned him. I finished my bite of donut. "Um, no."

She raised her eyebrows but remained silent. I washed sticky donut off my hands and then clapped them.

"All right, troops. Hazel, I need your phone to call the fire chief and see what I should do next. I have other calls to make too. Can you help the kids with a grocery list? Also, we need the internet turned on." I winked. "None of us will be happy without that."

Harry spoke up. "I can do whatever. Or I'll head back to the Center if you don't need me."

Work on the quetzals, he meant. How had I forgotten about them? Knowing Estelle used Gabby as her little pawn and finding out who killed Roger and Kurt didn't mean the mystery ended.

"I need you to find Stuart. We know Owen kidnapped him, but we haven't seen him since the marina. I want to know if he's all right. Also, remember when I asked you how you got the quetzals? We got interrupted. You mentioned you received a letter and came to Pensacola. What did the letter say?"

He pursed his lips. "I have it at my office if you want to see it. Basically, the Keatons asked if I'd be interested in researching the birds. I said yes." His eyes gleamed, and awe filled his voice. "It was the opportunity of a lifetime. They are near-threatened, which means they are likely to become endangered. I wanted to prevent that."

"I understand. Why didn't you ask the Keatons how they got the quetzals into the country?"

"They said they had permits and certificates to bring them here legally. I never asked to see them." He shrugged and heaved a sigh. "Honestly, after all of this, I can admit they weren't on the up and up. I knew it then, too, I suppose. I didn't want to pass up the chance."

I took the coin and the feather from his office even though that wasn't right. All in the name of 'research.' I wasn't any better than Harry. "'Pride goes before destruction, a haughty spirit before a fall,'" I said.

"Proverbs 16:18," Hazel said.

We exchanged glances. Time to fess up. "Before you beat yourself up too much, I took the feather and a coin from your office."

"I did too," Hazel confessed.

"Is that really the same as what I did?" Harry asked.

I rubbed my arms. It seemed like what he did was worse, but was it? "In God's eyes, I think what we are the same."

"Hmm."

That's all he said, so I dropped the subject. He wouldn't understand what I said if he didn't believe in God. I'd talk to him more about it later. He was one complex and odd man, but he had a vulnerability about him that drew me in. My kids would say he was another chick for me to take care of. They'd probably be right.

We went our separate ways. The kids headed out in the Bug to grocery shop, and Harry left to search for Stuart and then go to the Center. He wanted to check for more information about the quetzals' background. I was curious who supervised him and who he answered to in his research.

Hazel handed me a notepad and pen. "Make some lists. And here." She showed me a package of little sticky tabs. "You can use these for sections." She hugged me.

"You look exhausted," I said.

"I am. I'm not sure I've ever been tired like this before. I'm going to nap while you do your thing." She clicked her tongue at Roscoe and snapped her fingers for CB to follow her.

I started with a list of supplies we would need to live in her house. A small four-bedroom ranch with an open living, dining, and kitchen plan, it would be comfortable for us all. I closed my eyes and prayed, adding one for Marcus, wherever he was. I opened the news app on Hazel's phone, hoping for a report on the fire at the police station.

After scrolling halfway down my screen, I found what I was looking for. "Oh, my." I slapped my hand over my mouth. They mentioned my name in connection with the fire. My photograph appeared along with a Crime Stoppers Number.

I had joined the ranks of the Keatons.

"Okay, not looking for Marcus." I prayed he was safe and healthy, but if I looked for him now, I risked arrest. The police needed to find the bad guys—Owen and Gabby—not me.

I added restarting the internet to the first list. Hazel might have other companies to tell we were living in the house. I'd ask when she woke up.

Flip went that page, and I titled the next, 'What We Know.' Gabby confessed to killing Kurt—or whacking him, as she said. Owen offered up Estelle for Roger's murder. Or did he? I tapped the pen on my chin. I remembered one of them saying Roger was in the way and Estelle was bored with him. But they never explicitly said who killed him.

That went on a separate page—'What We Don't Know'—with asterisks beside it. Harry said the birds were worth more than the coins and that Estelle had given him both. She was the center of it all. Again.

"Ugh." I raked my hands through my hair. A door squeaked, and soft padding steps came down the hall. I turned, notebook raised, ready to fend off a bad guy. CB turned the corner from the bedrooms and trotted to me. I hugged him and stroked his soft fur. This guy comforted me in the way only he knew how. "You're my favorite. Don't tell Roscoe," I whispered in his ear.

Roscoe chose that minute to belt out, "Birds alive! Ta-da!"

"Shush, buddy." I dropped a treat in his cage. He'd bitten me enough times that I'd learned to keep my fingers away from his beak.

"Okay, back to my lists." I dropped into the chair, not knowing where to go from there. Birds and coins, coins and birds. Estelle. Who killed Roger? My brain needed time to process and sift through all I'd learned. Often, doing other things helped me.

All my insurance documents were at my house. I looked up my homeowner's insurance company on Hazel's phone, thankful she had a good data plan. The agent was kind, and when my voice and words got wobbly, she sympathized with me and steered me in another direction. Losing my house hadn't sunk in all the way. Zack and I raised our kids there, and it was where I lived after he died and where I started my blog, Mamma Birds.

That reminded me—had any of us worked on the blog recently? After the phone call ended, I had lots of confusing information, names, and phone numbers written down for adjustors and contractors. I took a break and opened up my blog admin page. Page views were lower than I'd ever seen them. My stomach sank. This was my livelihood, and Lauree had been too sick to contribute or be active on social media.

I spent an hour doing as much through Hazel's phone as possible. I added "buy a new laptop" to my list of things to purchase. The insurance agent explained some of the financial aspects, but most went in one ear and out the other.

I simply had too much to do.

Chapter 27

Cynthia tooted the Bug's horn, and I went outside to help carry the groceries inside. They purchased plenty of meat, bananas, apples, and fresh asparagus. I was surprised by how few junk food options they'd bought.

"You found some great choices." I held up a container of beautiful strawberries. "No more donuts for breakfast?"

Cynthia shook her head. "Nope. I'm going to practice on you guys. I've found some more healthy recipes that sound yummy."

Carter pulled out a sack of oysters. "She said she'd make Oysters Rockefeller tonight."

"One of my favorites," I said. I thought of the last time I ate Oysters Rockefeller at dinner with Shortie, and I turned away so they wouldn't see the pain on my face. Where did he and I stand? He spent his time restoring a car, but it felt like he had pulled away even more. I didn't want to seem needy, but I wanted at least some of his time.

The last time we'd talked had been at the motel. He'd promised to be there for me, but I never heard from him again.

Ugh. I didn't know what to do. My first choice would have

been to call Lauree, but I'd caused her enough stress. She didn't need to deal with my problems on top of hers.

Lord, please use this trial to heal my friend. I can live without her, but I don't want to.

Hazel came into the kitchen, her short hair stuck out in all directions. She yawned loudly, causing CB to bark and Roscoe to squawk.

"That's a way to make an entrance. Are you feeling better?" I worried about her. The last few days had been so hectic and scary. She was no spring chicken, and her face and posture showed exhaustion.

She smoothed her hair. "Yes, I slept so well. No bad dreams. I'm hungry now." She rooted through the items the kids had brought home. After a minute of looking, she chose bread, peanut butter, and jelly. "This is quick and easy. Anyone else up for a sandwich?"

We chatted while we ate. CB waited in hopes of a dropped bite or an on-purpose treat. I asked Hazel about any house services besides the internet that needed to be restarted. She had kept the power and water on since she moved in with me last year.

She still hadn't heard from Marcus, and I was worried. I didn't want to mention that my picture and the fire at the station were now on the news.

"My cell phone is gone. He told me to throw it away, and I did. I don't understand why he won't call you." I finished my sandwich and showed CB my empty hands. He moved over to sit by Cynthia and wagged his tail.

Hazel slid the notebook toward her and flipped through my notes. "Okay, Gabby killed Kurt," she read. "Um-hmm, yep, but no one ever copped to killing Roger."

"Copped, Grandma?" Carter teased. "You're learning the lingo."

She grinned and checked the rest of what I'd written. "Oh, Peg, I forgot all about the blog. It's not been long since you worked on it, right? Just a few days?"

I'd looked up the date when I signed into my admin page. "No, it's been weeks. The last time was when Cynthia came home and cooked breakfast for us."

"So, a month and a half?" Cynthia slipped CB a small bite of her sandwich and let him lick her fingers. "That's not too long."

In the blogging world, at least at the level of my Mamma Birds blog, regular posts and connecting through comments and social media were important. Essential, really. Readers go where they feel cared about. I cultivated my readership through the years, and I'd let them down.

The need to make decisions overwhelmed me.

"I'll have to talk to Lauree. We need to announce why things have been different. And I don't know ... how much Lauree will be able to do." There, I said it. I used to worry about whether I would be happy. Now, I wanted my best friend to be healthy. *Please, God, please.*

The four of us paused. Talking about Lauree left a pall over us. She would hate that.

"Everyone finished?" I asked. I gathered dishes, put food away, and washed up, Hazel by my side, not saying a word. Several months ago, she helped me figure out some things, like how to dream about the next stage in my life. Since that day, my life had done a one-eighty, and I was happy with a house full of people, animals, my blog, and new friends.

"I don't think I can do this without Lauree," I said, my voice filled with tears.

"Yes, you can. You won't want to, but you can." Hazel said. She hugged me and held on until I let go.

I grabbed a napkin and blew my nose.

"Mom?" Cynthia said. "I've consolidated all of what you wrote and made a list of what we still need to find out." She held up four fingers and counted down. "Who killed Roger Keaton? Where is his wife? How did the quetzals enter the country? How do the coins from the caravel figure into all of this?"

Carter brought his plate into the kitchen. "I have one more. Where is Marcus?"

Marcus. That's where we needed to start to solve all these questions.

HAZEL and I sent the kids to go buy us all some clothes. We could only do so much in a day, and we were all still worn out. Harry hadn't shown up, and Stuart and Marcus hadn't contacted us, so Hazel took another nap, and I used her phone to call Lauree.

"Where are you guys?" Lauree asked.

"Hazel's. We can stay here however long we need. It's fine."

"None of this is fine, Peg." Her voice trembled, and she sniffled.

"Please don't worry. It's bad for you." Guilt plagued me.

She caught her breath and snickered sarcastically. "*Cancer's* bad for you."

It was morbid humor, but this was where we were. "True. How are the kids? Have you and John talked to them?"

"We told them I'm sick, and I'll need extra help. They've been very sweet." She paused. "Are we safe at our house? Do you think whoever set your house on fire will come here?"

I hadn't had a chance to explain any of this to her.

"As far as I know, you are fine. If I hear different, you'll be the first to know." I tried to assure her we were doing everything possible to find the bad guys and filled her in on what we'd discovered and what Owen and Gabby had confessed to. I couldn't guarantee her family's safety. It infuriated me that I wasn't sure what would happen next. I listed the questions Cynthia had come up with. "Plus, we've had no word from Marcus or Stuart."

"I'm going to need a whiteboard for all of this." Paper rustled.

There she goes again, I thought. My friend was big on lists like Hazel. I waited as she mumbled under her breath. If only she could make sense of things and connect the dots. "Come up with any answers? We can use the help."

"Hang on." More mumbles followed, some scratching and a grunt. She cleared her throat. "I have a question. If Estelle gave Harry the coins when she gave him the quetzals, how did the coins come from the caravel?"

Huh? Smart woman.

I TAPPED on Hazel's bedroom door, heard a deep snort and a cough, and then, "Yes?"

I turned the knob and entered. "Just checking on you."

She waved her hand, turned over, and fell back to sleep. CB flopped his tail but kept his eyes closed. Poor things, catching up on the rest they had missed the last few days.

I called Harry and asked him about the connection between the coins and birds. "Did Estelle give you them at the same time?"

He hummed for a minute. "Yes ... I think so. Yes. Yes, she did."

Okay then. "You're sure?"

"I am. Why do you ask?"

I tapped my nails on the table and mulled over this new information. "All this time, we assumed the coins came from the caravel. Owen thinks so too. But Estelle had them in her possession long before the caravel's discovery—at least a month or more," I said.

"More like several months. We already have some eggs from the birds."

The sound of tires on the road and a horn honking caught my attention. "Where are you?"

"I'm almost to the fort to look for Stuart. I had to run a few errands before I headed there."

The kids came inside, laughing and chatting, and loaded down with their purchases. I waved and asked for the keys to the Bug.

"I'll be out there in about thirty minutes," I told Harry. "Together, we'll have a better chance of finding Stuart, although I'm not sure why he would be at the fort." I hung up and helped the kids sort out the clothes.

I picked up my stack. "I'm headed out to help Harry. How was shopping?"

"We had fun using your credit card." Cynthia chuckled.

"But please don't ask us to buy you underwear again, Mom." Carter made a face and pretended to shiver. "There are some things a guy doesn't need to know about his mother."

I winked and promised never to scar him again.

On my way out of the house, I called Marcus and got his voicemail. I left a long, convoluted message with what I knew and the connections I'd made.

Irritation sat in the back of my mind, just hanging out there. I refused to let it come out, and with all that had gone on the last few days, I'd done a good job. On my own for the first time in a long time—besides when I was in the motel—I thought about Shortie. By my count, I hadn't seen or talked to him in four days.

Not long ago, we hadn't gone more than twenty-four hours without checking in or getting together. Cynthia's question from this morning nagged at me, so I called him at the first stoplight I came to.

"Hey, Hazel." His cheery, carefree tone lit a fire inside of me.

"It's me." I hated how grumpy I sounded.

"Peg? Hi." He hesitated. "What's wrong?"

How did I answer his question? He had no idea what had transpired in my life the last several days. I shouldn't fault him for that.

Ugh. It stunk being mature.

I inhaled. "I'm home now."

"That's great. I can come by tonight." His eagerness to see me warmed me down to my toes.

"You can't come to my house." I exhaled.

"Why not?"

"It caught on fire." I was being mean and petty now. With some displaced anger even.

"What?"

I held the phone away from my ear at his screech. "Hang on." I pulled into the beach parking lot where Shortie had helped me search for Estelle's car not long ago. I parked and sighed.

"Peg," he growled, "what are you talking about?"

I told him. When I finished, it was quiet on his end.

"Shortie?"

"I'm not sure what to say." He cleared his throat. "Wow. Okay, first of all, are you all right? Are you and the kids and Hazel safe?"

My heart melted. He cared. He did. He simply hadn't been around.

Hmm. I'd think about that part later.

"I am safe. The kids and I are staying with Hazel at her house. Right now, I'm going to the beach to help Harry."

"Harry."

It wasn't a question. "Yes."

"What do you see in him, Peg?"

I couldn't do this right now. He may not have been aware of what I'd been through, and sure, he was catching up on it now, but Harry wasn't up for discussion.

"I need to go. I wanted to tell you where I was staying. I'll talk to you soon." I hung up and turned off the ringer.

Men.

I ARRIVED in the Visitor Center's parking lot and texted Harry. He messaged back that he was over the retaining wall near where we'd found the bloody tarp.

I traipsed through the parking lot, over the steps to the beach, and joined him. "You haven't seen Stuart anywhere?"

He shook his head. "You said you saw him scuffling with Owen?"

"That's what it looked like. He fell, and Owen tripped over him. They were fighting, but we were all running the other way, so I'm not positive what happened."

"What if he was in on it with Owen?" He flung his arms wide. "How much did Owen and Gabby tell us? Stuart is related to Gabby and Estelle. Owen's part of the 'gang.'" He made air quotes.

"What should we do then? Not worry about him? Assume he's with them? He didn't seem to be when we were at the marina."

"I think we need to go to the police department."

I shook my head. "Well, I can't do that."

"Why?"

"Harry, my picture is out there. I'm a wanted woman."

His lips twitched. Then the dimple peeked out. He bent over, shoulders shaking.

"Don't laugh. It's true." I stomped my foot, which, as it turned out, was not very effective in the sand.

He stood up, still laughing. "Oh, Peg. Oh, my." He held his belly.

I grinned. "Stop."

"I can't. I'm sorry." He drew in a deep breath. "Okay, okay." He cleared his throat. "I'm stopping." A chuckle popped out.

I shook my head, fists on my hips. "Are you?"

"Oh, boy. Wow. That felt good."

He was right. I giggled. It did feel good. We'd been through so much in the last few days. I slung my arm across his shoulders.

"Harry?"

"What?" He looked my way, eyes shining, dimple front and center.

I kissed his cheek. "You are one in a million."

"I know," he said.

Chapter 28

Stuart wasn't anywhere, and we didn't find any hints or clues to his whereabouts. We searched the treed area near the fort but were lost without knowing what to look for. The only positive thing was that we didn't find his body.

"I can call hospitals," I said once we circled back to our cars. "I'm not sure what his last name is, though."

"I'll go back to the marina and ask around." Harry volunteered.

I told him to find Ted Collins, who I thought was the unofficial head of the Society for Shipwrecks. He kept a boat at the marina. Harry went his way, and as I drove to Hazel's, I hopped off the interstate and went to West Florida Hospital to see if Stuart was there before I started making phone calls.

I entered the front sliding doors and spotted two uniformed police officers. Scooting behind a potted plant, I peeked out to see which way they were going. My photo was still out there with information to call Crime Stoppers. The short one talked about how Sharp's leg would heal, but he'd be off duty for a while.

Sharp? Was he talking about Marcus?

Had Marcus gotten hurt in the fire that Gabby started? The police officers wandered out the front door, and I bolted for the elevators. I backtracked to the receptionist to ask what floor he was on.

"Name?"

"Marcus Sharp." I kept my head down, hoping no one identified me through the security camera.

The receptionist typed his name in one letter at a time. "Yes, I see him. He's in room—" She paused and tapped another key. "Okay, here." She scribbled his room number on a slip of paper and handed it to me. I took it, grateful she didn't check if I was a relative. I'm not sure what I would say about that.

I rode the elevator to his floor, got off, and checked the hall, not wanting to run into any cops. I scurried down the hall, found his room, and ducked inside. The lights were off, but I could see his shape in the bed.

"Who's there?" he said.

"It's me," I whispered.

"Peg?" Marcus pushed himself up on his elbows. "Turn on the light."

I flipped it on and approached the bed. "That's quite a cast you have. What happened?"

He flopped back onto his pillow. "Well, let's see. I tried to keep you safe by sending you off by yourself. A fire broke out, and then I got trampled." He tapped his cast. "Two separate breaks, I'm told."

"Oh, Marcus, I'm sorry." I reached for his hand.

He rolled his eyes. "What are you sorry for? You got out just fine, I see. You've got yourself into a lot of trouble. I wanted to protect you. Keep you safe."

I jerked my hand back. "I didn't know what to do."

"So, you ran off? You need to turn yourself in." His harsh and grating words were valid, but I wanted to explain myself.

I met his eyes. "Marcus, it's not that easy. I didn't do anything wrong. You didn't arrest me. That guard you left for me? I don't know what happened, but someone else came to my door. I think I was set up."

He scratched the top of his thigh and tried to wiggle his pinky inside the cast. "How do you mean?"

Did he want to listen to me? That would be a first. I shifted on the bed. "Some man came to the motel and told me to leave. He took me around back, and Hazel was there."

"Hazel? How in the world did she know to be there?"

"Exactly," I said, eyebrows raised.

He rubbed his chin and scratched at the stubble on his face. I kind of liked the bearded look on him. It gave him even more of a brooding mystery-man vibe.

He crossed his arms. "Okay, I understand that you think you are innocent. But the point is the police want to talk to you. I need to call them right now. Convince me why I shouldn't."

How could I convince him? I didn't know what else to do to prove my innocence.

"How about the fire? Were you involved in that?" he asked.

"Of course not. Gabby confessed to it. You can ask Hazel, Carter, or Cynthia."

"How would they know?"

I told him the rest of what happened after I went home, complete with how Owen and Gabby tied us up.

His mouth dropped open. "Wait a minute, they had *all* of you?"

"Yes, it was Owen, Marcus. Owen. I never would've guessed he would do what he did." Tears filled my eyes and trickled down my cheeks. "Owen and Gabby tied up my kids, and then when Hazel and I arrived, they tied us up." This last part would be hard. I cleared my throat. "They also set my house on fire."

"What? They started a fire at your house and the police station?"

"Gabby confessed to setting the station on fire. Gabby and Owen were together at my house. One of them had put gasoline around it, and one of them lit it on fire." I recited the words like it had happened to someone else.

He narrowed his eyes. "That's quite the story."

Did he think I invented the whole thing? I remembered what he said when he first told me to stay somewhere besides my house. "You said someone tipped off the mayor?"

"Anonymous call. I looked into that. No proof." He winced.

"Are you hurting?"

He nodded. "Almost time for a pain pill. You should go so you're not caught." He patted the bed. "Move up here."

I scooted a little closer.

Marcus reached out his hand, and I took it. "Peg, I'm so glad you're all right."

His whispered words warmed my heart.

He tugged my hand, and I leaned over until we were nose and nose.

"A little closer," he said.

His kiss shot through me, all the way to my toes. I closed my eyes and leaned even closer. Warmth filled me—a different kind I hadn't experienced, at least not in the last dozen years. I pulled back and touched my lips.

His grin was cocky. "I've wanted to do that for a long time."

I remembered the one time he tried, and we were interrupted. That was months ago, and now I was with Shortie.

Shortie. "Oh, my."

Marcus winked. "Yep. Oh, my." He imitated my tone.

I wasn't saying it the way he thought. What had I done? I stood and backed away from the bed. "I need to go."

"Okay." His brows drew together, a question in his eyes.

"I'm sorry. Harry is supposed to look for Stuart, but he hasn't contacted me."

He picked up the remote to contact his nurse. He pushed the button and whispered, "Go."

He was letting me escape. I drew a shaky breath and stepped back. He must trust my story. Or else it was such a crazy mess he didn't know what to do with it.

No, Marcus always knew what to do. I touched my lips again.

The nurse responded to his call over the intercom, and he asked for more medication, his eyes still on me. I wiggled my fingers at him, turned, and hurried out of his room.

I didn't breathe easy until I was back in my car. He let me leave—*after* he kissed me. What a day.

I needed to see Lauree. She would ground me. Plus, she figured out the coins came before the caravel was discovered, so she might be able to make sense of the rest of this.

When I pulled into her driveway, she was watering her flowers. I avoided looking at my house. Instead, I studied my friend. She was a little thinner, and circles showed under her eyes in the porch light.

I got out and waved. She grinned and splashed me with the hose.

"Nice welcome." I laughed and dodged another spray.

She turned off the hose and curled it in a circle. "I'm so glad you're here." She gestured to the rockers.

We rocked and enjoyed the setting sun, the night air, and the cooler temperature. After several minutes, she spoke. "I'm sorry about your house."

"I'm sorry about your cancer." What was a house compared to the storm raging inside my friend? The house was fixable. I wasn't sure about Lauree.

She chuckled. "Me too. I have some news." She clasped her hands in her lap.

I attempted a normal response even as my heart raced. "Oh?"

"We got a call yesterday. There's an experimental drug, and I'm a candidate for the trial. I start next week." She looked at me. Her eyes glimmered in the fading light.

"Oh!" Tears welled in my eyes. "That's good news? Right?"

"I think so. I'm excited about it." She sat back and sighed. "I never imagined any of this." She gestured to herself.

"Yeah."

"I suppose you never imagined your life this way either?"

I sniffled and wiped my face. "No, but you know what?" I squeezed her hand where it lay on the rocker's arm. "I wouldn't trade my life for anything."

She squeezed back. "Me either."

SUNDAY MORNING DAWNED cloudy and overcast. Thunder rumbled in the distance. After showering, I sorted through the clothes my kids had bought and pulled on dark blue Bermuda shorts and a bright orange T-shirt. Not a color I typically wore, but it would do for whatever the day would bring.

I started the coffee and stirred up pancake batter. CB wandered into the kitchen, and I tossed him a blueberry. He caught it but spit it back out, then sat and looked at me.

"Not a fan, huh?" I picked up the berry and tossed it in the trash. "What if I make bacon?"

He woofed.

"Funny boy." Hazel's phone rang. 'Unknown Caller' appeared on the screen. My stomach rolled. Was it Estelle Keaton on the other end? I hit the answer and speaker buttons. "Yes."

"Hey, Peg. It's me." Harry's voice settled my hackles.

"Hey, I texted you last night, but you didn't respond. Are you okay?"

He cleared his throat. "That's what I'm calling about."

His tone sounded off. I strained to hear any background noises. "Are you still at the marina?"

"Sure am. When ya comin' to see me?" He chuckled, but in a manner I never heard from him.

Harry didn't say things like that. He didn't even say, "y'all."

The hair on the back of my neck rose. "Would you like me to come there?" Please say no, please say no. I just wanted a normal life where the biggest choice to make was whether I cooked bacon or not, and no one set my house on fire, one where I knew for sure if I was in love with Shortie or Marcus.

Ugh. I tuned back into Harry.

"Yes, come on over. I've been here all night." He grunted. "Okay, okay," he whispered.

I strained to hear more. Someone was with him. "Sure, I'll be there soon."

"Come alone, Peg," he said in a serious tone.

Hazel wandered into the kitchen as I clicked off the phone call. "I think your pancakes are burning."

I grabbed the skillet and dropped it in the sink, where it sizzled and popped. I stuck the bowl of batter in the refrigerator. "Harry called. He sounded strange. Something is up with him."

She poured herself a cup of coffee. "Where was he?"

"The Blue Oyster Marina. I think he's in trouble. He said 'ya' and 'comin'.' He doesn't talk like that."

Hazel's eyes widened. She set her mug on the counter. "Well, what are you waiting for? We have to go."

Harry said to come alone, but I knew better. No matter what happened between Marcus and me, I needed to tell him what I planned to do. I texted the information and told him what Harry said, and Hazel and I left.

We pulled into the marina's parking lot just as the rain started falling. Without knowing where Harry was, I thought we could go out on the back deck where we first found the Society for Shipwrecks group. We entered the front door, and it was dark, like before. Thunder rumbled outside, and lightning lit up the lobby area.

Hazel led the way to the back deck. This time, the double glass doors were shut and locked.

"Any other ideas?" she said.

I shook my head. "All he told me was he was at the marina. He might be anywhere, even outside."

"Let's check inside the building before we go out there." A lightning bolt streaked across the sky, and another clap of thunder sounded, reinforcing Hazel's idea.

Behind us, someone cleared his throat, and I turned. "Owen?"

"Hello, Peg, Hazel. Are you looking for Harry? Did you ever find Stuart?" Owen was alone this time, with no gun in sight.

"No, I don't know where either man is. Where is Gabby?" I edged closer to my mother-in-law.

He leaned against the wall and shrugged. "No idea."

How was he so casual about this? He'd held my family and me hostage, tied us up, and left us to die.

"Marcus knows we were coming here," I said.

He pushed off the wall. "Now, Peg, let's not blow this all out of proportion. You're making too much of what happened.

I'm sorry if we've lost our friendship, but you can see how wrong you are, right?"

How wrong *I* was? I looked at Hazel, and she shook her head.

"He's lost his mind," she muttered.

Owen stepped closer. "You have to understand that woman—the Keaton woman—made me do everything. Remember last year when the mayor was the stool pigeon? That's what happened to me."

I cocked my eyebrow. "You're the stool pigeon." He didn't miss my sarcastic tone.

Chapter 29

He huffed. "That's not what I meant." He held out his hand. "Come on. We can get past this, right? You see what I'm saying? That I wasn't at fault?"

I grabbed Hazel's hand and backed away from him. He circled around and stopped with his back to the glass doors.

"You shouldn't be afraid of me."

My mouth dropped open. "You held a gun on us. You tied us up and left us to die." Anger vied with disbelief, and my words ended in a growl.

I jumped at the sound of thunder booming overhead. Glancing outside, I saw lightning strike one of the trees, snapping off a thick branch. The boats docked at the marina pitched in the strong winds and choppy water, and trees beside the deck blew back and forth.

"Peg?" Harry called out. He rounded the corner and skidded to a halt.

"Come over here, Harry." I waved him to my side.

He hurried to me, avoiding Owen. "I found Stuart. He's in a room, and so is Gabby." Harry swallowed, his Adam's apple bobbing like the boats outside. "They're both unconscious."

His words lit another fire—one inside my head, and the words popped out, "Owen Walters, what in the world have you done?"

"He grabbed me as soon as I arrived. He tied me up, but I broke free." Harry held up his wrists, showing us the bruises.

"You don't believe him, do you, Peg?" Owen tipped his head. "Think of all the fun times we've had, us and the birding group."

He reached into his pocket and pulled out a key ring. He found the key he wanted and grabbed the door handle. Before he could unlock it, lightning struck the glass doors, shattering them. Shards flew inside, helped along by the strength of the strike and the heavy winds. Hazel, Harry, and I turned and crouched away from the damage, covering our faces and heads. A loud grunt followed by a scream made me turn.

A large chunk of the glass door pinned Owen to the opposite wall. A piece of the handle was buried in his thigh, and his face bled from multiple gouges. He reached out his hand.

"Peg? Please, help me."

I studied my former friend and thought about the birding trips we'd been on, how he helped me find the proper boots so my feet would be safe, and how he introduced us to Dr. Maggie Turnball. I wouldn't go near the man, but I could use this time to ask questions.

"Where's Estelle Keaton?"

He made a face. "I don't know. She's the one at fault, though. You have to understand." He closed his eyes and groaned.

I raised my eyebrows and kept quiet.

"I have no idea where she is, I promise." He whimpered.

Outside, the storm continued its damage. Another band of heavy rain fell, spraying us all through the broken doors. A waterspout appeared and skipped across the water, destroying several boats and a dock. I braced. Did we need to search for cover in an interior room? I breathed a sigh of relief when the spout disappeared into the dark clouds.

Owen cried out and reached for the door handle stuck in his leg.

"You better not pull that. You'll bleed out. You won't get any sympathy from us," Hazel chimed in. She shook her head and stomped her foot. "You are a bad man. I cannot believe I thought I loved you."

Owen moved his hand. "I thought I loved you, too, dear." His smile was smarmy. "In fact, I wanted to ask you out on a date."

"*Pfft.*" She shook her finger at him, her eyes narrowing. "You are a liar. *Dear.*"

If looks alone could kill, the glass would not just pin Owen, he would've caught on fire too. Speaking of fires ...

"Time to fess up." Sirens sounded, and the front doors of the building crashed open.

Owen squirmed and tugged, attempting to free himself. Every move he made increased the bleeding and caused him extreme pain, judging by his groans and screams.

Police officers approached, weapons drawn. One said, "Peg Howard, I'm looking for her."

I raised my hand.

"Mrs. Howard, Detective Sharp informed us you would be here."

I closed my eyes, my heart shattering like the glass doors. Marcus had turned me in. I couldn't believe it, especially after our kiss. I held out both arms, wrists together, and waited for the cold snap of handcuffs. When nothing happened, I opened my eyes.

The officer tipped his head, eyebrows drawn together. "He

said we needed to find an Owen Walters?" He looked between Harry and Owen. "Which one of you is that?"

We all pointed at Owen and said in unison, "Him."

Owen glared, his lip curling. "I didn't do anything. They've got it all wrong."

I held up my hand, fingers spread. "One, he killed Roger Keaton."

"No, Estelle did that," Owen spluttered. He whined and complained while I kept talking.

"Fine. Two, he kidnapped Stuart. He's in a room here. Gabby is too. Plus, Gabby started the fire at the police station, so you'll want to arrest her." I tapped my finger on my chin. "What else am I forgetting?"

By this time, Owen was handcuffed, and a policewoman read him his rights.

"The fire at your house," Hazel said.

"Yes, three. He and Gabby started a fire and tried to burn down my house."

Two emergency medical technicians hurried into the hallway. They spotted Owen handcuffed and still pinned to the wall by the chunk of glass. The female EMT stared open-mouthed. "Are you kidding me? What happened here?"

OWEN BLABBED his whole confession right there. Not the smartest move. He confessed to kidnapping Harry and Stuart and tying up me, Hazel, and my kids, but he continued to accuse Estelle Keaton of killing her husband. He said all that before they took him to the hospital for his injuries. The police assured me that he would go to jail once he recovered. He was no longer a threat, thank goodness.

It had been weeks since I felt safe.

Based on my testimony, they arrested Gabby. Both she and Owen would have a trial, and Hazel, Harry, and I would have to testify.

It didn't escape my notice that Estelle Keaton remained on the loose. I had plenty of questions to ask her. If she was found. The police were looking for her but hadn't seen her yet.

And I still didn't know who my motel mystery man was.

The thunderstorm passed while Hazel, Harry, and I made our statements at the police station. I was no longer a suspect. I got my keys and drove to Hazel's on autopilot, thinking through all that had taken place up to now and what I still needed to do. Reese was almost one month old. I met Harry. Hazel and I investigated the quetzal mystery and ended up almost being killed. It seemed like a lifetime had taken place in the last four weeks. I parked in Hazel's driveway and enjoyed a few extra quiet moments, knowing my kids would have a billion questions when I went inside.

The mound of errands and tasks to do piled up. Besides getting my house cleaned and inspected, Carter and Cynthia needed new cars.

I entered the house and set down the keys. Voices came from the living room. I found Hazel, Harry, Cynthia, and Carter seated on the couches. CB snuggled against Hazel's legs and wagged his tail when he saw me. Roscoe chirped my way.

"You've had a long day," Cynthia said. She handed me a bottle of water.

"Thanks." I unscrewed the top and drank half of it. "Whew, that is good." I sat between my kids and hugged them to me.

"Grandma told us about Mr. Owen. I can't believe all the things he did." Carter shook his head.

"Gabby and Stuart should be fine. They'll recover at the hospital and answer a lot of questions. He might be more involved than we know." I sipped more water. "Gabby confessed that she killed Kurt and started both fires. She'll go to jail from the hospital, and we may have to testify about that."

"No problem," Cynthia said.

Hazel leaned forward, eyes narrowed. "I'll testify against Owen. What a snake."

I felt terrible that, at one time, she and I both suspected Harry of being involved. "Does Carmen know what happened? She's the one birder I haven't talked to." I stretched out my legs with a contented sigh.

Hazel shook her head. "I haven't talked to her, either. We still haven't answered two questions." She scratched CB's ears.

"Where did the quetzals and the coins come from?" Cynthia said.

"And where is Estelle? No one ever sees her," I said.

Harry frowned. "The quetzals came from Guatemala. Remember, I told you she sent me a letter. And she gave me the coins."

"Somehow, she started the rumor about the curse and made everyone think the coins came from the caravel." I recalled what Owen told us when Hazel and I were at his house. "Owen fanned those flames, too, didn't he?"

Hazel nodded. "We never found out if the coins are real or not."

"Do you think she tricked me? She told me the coins were very valuable and would fund my research." Harry's expression was pained.

"Some of this we may never find out, but it sounds like she tricked you and Owen," I said. Estelle Keaton was slippery. She'd disappeared last year and reappeared this time with the quetzals. We might never know how and where she got the coins, and I didn't care as much anymore.

I patted my legs and stood. "I am going to shower and go to

bed. Tomorrow is a new day, and we can put all this behind us."

~

I OPENED my eyes to see flames shooting up the wall. Pictures melted, and the dresser caught on fire. I couldn't move. My hands were cuffed to the bed. I opened my mouth to scream, but no words would come out. This time, I wouldn't escape.

I was going to die.

Someone shook my shoulder, and I sprang up in my bed.

"Peg, you were screaming. It's okay. You're all right. You were dreaming." Hazel sat beside me and brushed the hair from my face.

I looked around my room. "No fire," I whispered.

"No, dear. You're safe in my house. No fire."

I sank back into my pillows. "These nightmares are making me crazy."

She rubbed my arm. "Come on, get up. I'm sure you're hungry."

Hunger didn't cause bad dreams, but I didn't argue with her. I pulled on my robe. Coffee would help wake me up, and breakfast didn't sound too bad either. My stomach rumbled in response to my thoughts.

Hazel handed me a mug filled to the brim. I settled down at the table. Carter opened the front door, and CB bounded into the house. Carter let go of the leash.

"Walking him is like handling the Tasmanian Devil." He handed Hazel several envelopes. "Here's some mail, Grandma."

I called the dog and unhooked his leash. "I'm not sure I've ever walked him. He once came to the beach with me, but he behaved very well."

Carter rolled his eyes. On the hearth, Roscoe piped up, "Ta-da!"

"How come you have mail here?" I asked.

Hazel shrugged. "It's mostly junk mail. Oh, and here, a letter from the neighborhood association." She ripped open an envelope and scanned the paper before handing it to me.

"What's this?"

She pointed to it. "Read it. I've found us another bird mystery to solve."

"Nope, not me. No more mysteries. I'm done." I set the letter down and wiped my hands together.

She picked it up and handed it to me again. "Read it."

I sighed. She wouldn't quit until I did what she said. I read the letter aloud, "To the residents of Stone Creek Cove." I looked at her. "I didn't realize your neighborhood had a name. Very nice."

She cocked an eyebrow.

I cleared my throat and started again. "To the residents of Stone Creek Cove. Please be advised that we are in contact with the police about a recent theft. The snowy egret colony in our neighborhood creek is missing. If you know of anyone involved in this, contact us or the police. They have suggested we install security cameras on each side of the creek and along the walking trail. Be advised—we will not put up with losing our egrets."

I set down the letter. "Someone stole an entire colony of birds? How do they know they didn't fly away?"

"No, someone stole them. We have always had lots of the little guys in the creek area. They're beautiful. All white with skinny black legs and yellow feet. And now, they're gone. We have no egrets."

Carter slapped his leg. "Funny, Grandma. No egrets, get it? No regrets?"

I giggled at his silliness. "I don't see how we can help with this. They may have flown somewhere for the summer. I don't want to solve any more mysteries, Hazel. Even if it's just a few missing birds. Don't you think we've had enough drama?"

"It's more than a few missing birds!" She threw her hands in the air. "They are part of the ecosystem. Carter, back me up on this."

He shrugged. "She has a point."

"I'm sure this is important, but I don't want to investigate anymore." I had enough to solve in my own life, let alone search for some white birds. And, like I said, I was tired of drama.

Hazel retrieved her notebook from her room. "I'll just make a few notes, okay? We'll see where it takes us."

I grimaced. She was like a bulldozer. Carter chuckled and repeated his corny "no regrets" joke.

The doorbell rang. I was still laughing when I opened it. I stopped when I realized who it was and what he was doing.

There on the front porch was Shortie, kneeling on one tuxedo-clad knee, holding out a small, square open box containing a gorgeous white gold band with a single, teardrop-shaped diamond. Tears burned the back of my eyes. I met his gaze, his gray eyes alight with a fire I had never seen. I resisted straightening his crooked bowtie.

"Peg." My name came out husky. "I love you. I've loved you for months, and when I thought I would lose you, I finally realized it. Please marry me and make me the happiest man alive."

My hand went to my mouth. He said those three little words. But could I say them back? I thought of Marcus's kiss from two days earlier and what I had told Chloe several weeks ago, 'Shortie and I just happened.' I knew I was comfortable with and cared about him, but I wasn't sure that was enough. Then I remembered how he questioned my feelings for Harry.

I didn't know what to say.

A police car pulled into the driveway. Shortie stood and turned. The passenger door opened, and one leg appeared, followed by a cast and two crutches. Marcus stood, got his bearings with the crutches, and headed our way.

I looked between the two men. What to do, what to do? I sighed loudly, backed up, stepped inside the house, and closed the door.

"What are you doing? Who was at the door?" Hazel asked.

I sat at the table and pulled the letter toward me. "No one. So, what do you think we should do about this? We can't live with no egrets."

The End

Acknowledgments

To my critique groups, Scribes 201 and Word Weavers Page 19, thank you for your friendship and amazing critiques. You rock!

About the Author

Jen Dodrill, retired Navy wife and homeschool mom, is living out her dreams on the pages of her books, bringing readers compelling stories of inspiration and hope for good times and bad.

Her family-focused novels depict her values of cooperation, connection, compassion, and community, demonstrating the importance of helping one another brave the waves of the world together.

As a mother of five, family life and travels have left her with decades of stories to tell, and she cherishes the time she has now to tell them, in between her honored role as Grandma, her passion for reading, and her adoration of all things coffee.

For more information about Jen, her books, writing tips, and author interviews, check out her blog:

https://jendodrillwrites.com.

Also by Jen Dodrill

Birds Alive

An Empty-nesters Mystery—Book One

Peg—widow, mom blogger, and empty nester—is desperate for a new hobby. After a late-night blog post leaves her dedicated Mamma Birds followers fearful that she's closing her blog, she adopts a reader's suggestion and forms the Empty Nesters Birding Group. On their first outing overlooking beautiful Pensacola Bay, a birder dies from an allergic reaction to peanuts in the birdseed. Seed that should be peanut-free.

A hurricane barrels toward the Gulf Coast, and Peg's overbearing, animal-collecting, but well-meaning mother-in-law crashes Peg's empty nest. After the hurricane passes, Peg checks on her new birder friends and finds one wounded and dying. The assailant is still there and knocks Peg down a steep staircase. Stuck in a boot with a broken foot and still reeling from the two murders, Peg recruits a fellow birder and her mother-in-law to help solve the crime. She even teams up with the detective investigating the case, whose dimples draw her in a way she hasn't experienced in years.

Get your copy here:

https://scrivenings.link/birdsalive

You May Also Like ...

The Case of the Stolen Memories

A Mac & Sam Mystery—Book Three

It's the beginning of a new year and Private Investigator Mackenzie Love resolves to get in better shape. But after only one week of walking before work, she interrupts a burglary in progress and ends up in the middle of a murder case.

Detective Jake Sanders, the man Mac's dating, is assigned to the murder, and Mac, along with her partners Samantha Majors and Ms. Prudence Freebody, are hired to find the memorabilia stolen from the time capsule in Rennick Park. The two cases intertwine, and Mac finds herself once more on the wrong end of a gun!

Can Mac and Jake find the killer and the stolen property before the killer finds them?

Get your copy here:

https://scrivenings.link/stolenmemories

Best Seller by Christina Rost

An H&G Mystery—Book One

When crime fiction novelist Kelly Landon agrees to write a memoir for an eccentric, elderly gentleman, her quiet life turns upside-down.

Unbeknownst to her, the memoir is peppered with clues leading to a rare collection of stolen jewels from World War II. After the memoir makes the best-seller list, Kelly finds herself in the crosshairs of a decades-old vendetta.

Now, instead of enjoying her rise to literary fame, she's thrust into the dangerous world of treasure hunting.

While Kelly struggles to win the game of cat-and-mouse, a secret family legacy is unearthed, forcing her to choose between trusting her charming literary agent or her vigilant bodyguard to keep her safe.

As the three of them become entangled in a web of deceit, it's a race to see who's the villain, who's the hero, and who holds all the pieces to solve the mystery of the best seller.

Get your copy here:

https://scrivenings.link/bestseller

Stay up-to-date on your favorite books and authors with our free e-newsletters.

ScriveningsPress.com